I0773394

PHICKSHUN

TIM MILLER

GP

GNATCATCHER
PRESS

Hey Ben. I know the copyright of my third book might not be the best place for this, but I wanted to let you know that I saw the video where you put the jalapeños (and not my second book) in Marty's sandwich. Hilarious. And that he had to order milk, which came in a carton that he struggled to open, is plain awesome. I appreciate a good sandwich hijinks as much as the next person, but if we could get serious for a moment: Copyright laws are, unlike our college acapella group the Fresh Sheets, no laughing matter. I don't want you to get busted. Because I also talked to Kevin. And he told me that you put "Reading Ketchup" in his pastrami on rye. Listen, I know you have a penchant for messing with lunch orders, but I can't give you my consent. If you're circulating my book inside sandwiches, you're breaking the law. I think the best thing is for you to stop. Please. Before things get out of hand.

Cover design by Jessica Bell
Interior design by Amie McCracken

ALSO BY TIM MILLER:

Spooves
Reading Ketchup

To Megan

*The artist must know the manner whereby
to convince others of the truthfulness of his lies.*
—Pablo Picasso

TABLE OF CONTENTS

PHICKSHUN

A bell rings. You are in a classroom. You feel a mix of excitement and nervousness. It's your first day of high school.

A teacher stands in the front of the room. The expectant faces around you all look up. They are new and familiar at the same time. It's either the first time you are seeing them or the first time you are seeing them in years. There is the feeling of newness, a beginning, but also familiarity, déjá vú. You've been here before, but something is different.

You look down and recognize the same clothes you wore on your first day. It all comes back.

The English teacher is male. He was not your freshman year teacher. He's a stranger, part of the uncertainty, out of place with everything else. You have a distinct feeling that he doesn't belong. He has long, thick, blond curly hair tied in a ponytail. He is young, muscular. He wears khaki pants, a royal blue button-down shirt, a navy blue tie with golden horizontal stripes. The knot is loose and his first button is undone. He hasn't shaved in a couple days. He has a square jaw.

Using a green dry erase marker, he writes his name on the whiteboard: Mr. Bigfatliar. Then in large capital letters, in the center of the board, he writes: PHICKSHUN.

He turns and looks at the class.

That's when you notice something is off. His eyes. They're a little crossed. He starts talking. His voice is strange, garbled. Almost like an echo. Far-away sounding. And there's another thing: His words don't exactly match his moving lips. There's a slight delay.

"Art is a lie that tells the truth."

He repeats the quote slowly, emphasizing *lie* and *truth*. Then he turns and writes the quote on the board, right underneath PHICKSHUN. He underlines lie and truth. Then he smiles and you notice that he has braces. Or you think he has braces. Those invisible adult ones. He keeps making small slurping sounds, like he has an issue with saliva.

He starts speaking again, slowly walking around the room. The slurping morphs into a lisp.

"I'm going to tell you about a writer. To graduate college this writer had to write a five-page paper on that quote, 'Art is a lie that tells the tells the tells the truth' and three other pieces of art. A book, a poem, and a painting. The book was *Invisible Cities* by Italo Calvino. The poem was 'Kubla Khan.' And the painting was the painting was the painting was—"

He jerks his head, swinging his ponytail across his back.

"*Guernica* by Pablo Picasso." He flicks his tongue to both corners of his mouth. It's fleeting, but you catch a glimpse. It's dark purple, almost black, with a forked tip.

"This student, a journalism major, harbored dreams of becoming a writer. But picture him, sitting in a basement computer lab. It's well past midnight. And he's totally stuck. He has zip. Five pages to go… the question remains, What does the quote actually mean?"

The teacher walks past you and you hear a low sound, like a whirring of gears, the humming of a machine. He talks again, approaching. You notice the tip of his tie is frayed. Now he is walking away from you. You look at the heels of his brown shoes. His khaki pants are wrinkled at the cuff. He starts talking again. The student next to you is chewing gum and pops a bubble. Many of the students in the room, you notice, are not listening. They are doodling in their notebooks or just staring at the floor.

"The quote is a paraphrase from a Pablo Picasso letter in 1923. What he actually wrote is, 'We all know Art is not Truth. Art is a lie that makes us realize truth.' He goes on to say, 'The artist must know the manner whereby to convince others of the truthfulness of his lies.'"

He is back at the board. He writes, fast, slashing with the marker. There is a hint of violence in each letter.

Fiction is Art.

Fiction, by definition, is not true.

For fiction to be any good, it must be true.

You begin to take notes, but your pen is leaky. The ink flows out erratically, making blotchy letters that you smear with your wrist.

He turns and now is wearing glasses. Where did the glasses come from? There are sounds from the hall. An authoritative voice talking on a walkie-talkie. There is another sound, like the distant blades of a helicopter. Then, very distinctly, the sound of a goat.

You look up and the glasses melt on the teacher's face. His eyes are hard-boiled eggs. The teacher falls on his face and starts crackling and hissing. You can see the circuitry along the back of his neck, the wires that hold his limbs.

Everything around you collapses, as if it's all two-dimensional cardboard.

You sit, surrounded by white nothing. For a distinct moment you feel a sense of disappointment, like you've been cheated. The teacher was going somewhere, and you wanted to go there, for both the ride and the destination. And now you see that there was no there there. Whatever it was, dream or memory, contained a flaw in the design. Then you feel a pang of sadness. Like maybe there *was* something there. A grain of human experience, either funny or beautiful or quirky. Small and intangible, but not insignificant. Like a fond memory of a person or a place that you carry in the pocket of your mind. And that maybe, with a little more time or skill, maybe…

Then you see that the white wall in front of you is actually a blank page, one you can turn.

HAPPY BIRTHDAY

Makeesha was thinking she should spoil herself and go shopping. It was her twenty-second birthday. In a month she would be graduating with a degree in graphic design. She didn't have a job lined up, but she did have a couple of promising internship applications pending with marketing departments. Still, it was her birthday. She deserved this.

First, she decided to find a graduation dress. She was thinking something formal that she could also wear out. She tried on a pink dress but it didn't fit her quite right. Then she tried on a blue dress and a red dress. She liked them equally and after debating for a moment decided to buy both. Why not?

Then she bought a pair of shoes that matched both dresses, some underwear, and a top. She was thinking about her dinner that evening with her boyfriend Don and whether he might propose. She thought about what kind of husband he would make and the way she would say yes. She even rehearsed her expressions in the fitting room mirror. Surprise! Beaming joy. A mischievous glint. Love. She was thinking that she was ready for marriage and that she and Don will have been together two and a half years next month. It was time, she thought.

He was a lifeguard and was taking classes to become an EMT. His ultimate goal was to become a firefighter. It was extremely competitive to become a firefighter in Southern California, but Makeesha never thought about those kinds of odds. Instead, she thought about how Don would make a great husband. In the fitting room she was thinking about him as a firefighter. And their life together. She was thinking how many kids she might want and how many Don might want. She thought about that time at the beach when they talked about one day starting a family and he had said yes, he wanted kids.

"Two? Maybe three?" he had said with a shrug and a smile.

And how many years should they wait after getting married? They didn't talk about that. She was thinking at least three. It would depend on their jobs. But that was at the edge of her thoughts as she put her T-shirt back on and left the fitting room to pay for the top.

She picked up some makeup that she needed and stopped for coffee to answer all the texts and posts on her phone. After the coffee, she went and had her hair and nails done. While she was getting a shampoo she felt a little guilty about not bringing her mom or her sister or any of her friends along shopping, but she needed some alone time. That was when she decided to get her nails done too. She was thinking how nice it was to go shopping just by herself.

After her nails were done she went home. She lay down and, before she knew it, fell asleep. She had a short dream where she was already married and pregnant when Don died fighting a fire. It was a dream she had had before, and she didn't think too much about it as she brushed her teeth. Instead, she thought about which dress she should wear to dinner and whether she still had time to take her pug Lulu for a walk. Which reminded her. She called Don.

Don had gone out the night before with his buddies Crew and Collin. They had stayed up late playing a drinking game called "cups." He was thinking he was getting a little old to be playing drinking games, especially this morning when he awoke fifteen minutes before noon with a splitting headache. He had a hair-of-the-dog beer with a breakfast burrito, took two Advils, and smoked a bowl with his roommate Reed. He knew he might have to take a drug test if his application came through to begin his EMT training course—but that hadn't happened, and besides, Crew had passed his with a drink you could buy. As he put on his wet suit and grabbed his surfboard, he was thinking that he had to live his life while he was young.

He went and surfed for an hour. There was not a speck of cloud in the sky. He was just thinking about the waves and surfing the whole time. Sometimes he would sit on his board and think about Makeesha, a beautiful girl out there who was maybe thinking about him, too.

The waves were waist-high and steady. He could've stayed there until sunset, but he knew he had Makeesha's birthday dinner. He drove home and took a short nap and didn't dream. He woke up to his phone buzzing. It was Makeesha wondering if he had made a reservation. He hadn't thought of that. But he did some quick thinking and suggested Bert's Café in La Jolla, a place he knew she loved because Lulu could sit on the patio.

"If there's a wait we could have a drink at the bar," he said.

"Okay," she said. "And what did you decide about my aunt's?"

Don had forgotten: Makeesha wanted him to go up to Orange County with her and spend the night at her aunt's. Her aunt was throwing a birthday/early graduation party for Makeesha on Sunday. But Don had to work the dawn shift on Monday morning at Torrey Pines State Beach. They had argued about it a week ago to no avail and ended up dropping it.

"Babe, listen…" he said.

They started to argue again, but then Makeesha said, "Whatever. I don't want to fight anymore. Let's just drive separately and meet at the restaurant because I'll have to leave right from dinner."

Makeesha put on her new underwear, new makeup, new red dress, and new shoes. She liked how she looked in the mirror. She grinned and thought, Don better propose soon.

She drove south from Pacific Beach to La Jolla, listening to P!nk and Andy Grammer and singing along. She petted Lulu and didn't think much of anything at all. It was a short drive but the traffic was, as she texted Don while driving, *ridic*. She turned up the volume, singing off-key about how good it was to be alive.

She couldn't find a parking spot on the street, so she turned and parked in the La Jolla Village Shopping Center across the street from the restaurant. She parked, put Lulu on her leash, and got out of the car.

*

Don put on a button-down shirt and jeans, thinking his shirt was a little wrinkled. He looked in the mirror and thought he could use a shave. But he saw there wasn't time. He thought he should start shaving more and getting his shirts dry-cleaned.

He drove north from Ocean Beach to La Jolla. The traffic from the south was light, and he found parking surprisingly quickly on the street right in front of the restaurant. He went into Bert's Café and put down his name. Party of two. It was crowded and there would be a thirty-minute wait. He saw Makeesha's text so he knew he had some time before she arrived. He decided to pick up some flowers at the grocery store in the La Jolla Village Shopping Center across the street. He walked over and bought some yellow daffodils, her favorite.

*

He was holding the flowers outside the grocery store when he saw her park in the shopping center parking lot. He watched her get out with Lulu on her leash. He enjoyed watching her without her knowledge. She held the leash loosely, and Lulu dashed and almost got away from her. He kept offering to train the dog but she always refused. She was stubborn that way, he thought. She looked very beautiful, and he thought she was wearing a new dress and had her hair done. He remembered his sister telling him how important it was for boyfriends to notice that stuff.

The parking lot was very busy. Lulu strained the leash as they walked. A car backed out suddenly and Lulu almost got run over. Makeesha stopped and disappeared from Don's view as the car pulled away.

Then the car drove off and she was walking again. She looked down at her phone and slowed to send a text message. She looked up and saw him and waved. He stood and watched the way her dress and her hair moved in the wind and thought the same thoughts as from the ocean earlier.

She stopped to look back at her phone as if to respond to something and then looked back at him, walking again. She lifted her sunglasses onto the top of her head and they looked at each other. She saw the flowers and smiled. He could see the smile was in spite of their argument. Like she wanted to restrain it, but she also didn't. Like, how could she be mad at him? There was a slight tilt and shake of the head, a squint of an eye. And that smile. She's beautiful, he thought, as she crossed the street, her outline threaded by the light of the setting sun.

*

Bill was thinking about the Dodgers lineup as he loaded the Garda armored vehicle with three bags full of cash from the Wells Fargo Bank. It was a good lineup, he thought, but they needed their third baseman Turner back. He drove along listening to the Dodgers-Pirates pregame show and turned into the La Jolla Shopping Center. He stopped in front of the CVS, went in, and picked up one bag of cash and one of coins. Seventeen down and three to go, he thought.

He loaded the bags, not thinking about the rest of his route or his problems with his older son that was getting in trouble in middle school or the way his wife had seemed distant of late. He wasn't thinking about any of the things that had been keeping him up at night, including the lurid and vivid dreams he had been having lately about his father and the recent discovery of a cyst on his father's liver that had been putting pressure on his heart. That morning his father had just been released from the hospital in Lexington, Kentucky, after having over seven liters of fluid drained from his body. In the morning, Bill had thought about seven liters abstractly while pouring orange juice at breakfast, but he hadn't thought about it since. As with so many things lately, he shoved it to the back of his mind, like a cluttered drawer that won't close.

He got back in the truck and waited for the traffic to clear. There was a commercial on the radio. He was thinking about his dinner and if he should pick something up or just stop and eat on his own somewhere. His wife had taken the kids to her mom's, so he knew he was eating on his own; it was just a matter of where. It might be nice to eat at a bar and watch the Dodgers. But it would be nice to watch the game at home, too.

Well, he had three stops to decide. He was tired and he was close to the end of his shift. This particular week had been a rough one for his insomnia. He could never fall back asleep when he awoke in the night. It was frustrating just lying there, sleep a fortress that wouldn't let him in. He was thinking it would be nice to finish work today and then have two days off. To get some sleep.

He wasn't really thinking too hard about anything as the traffic cleared. He listened to the radio and pulled away from the CVS. The Dodgers were 8—11 on the 2018 Major League baseball season and the commentators were discussing if the slow start was cause for Dodgers fans to worry.

But he wasn't really listening and he wasn't really worried about the Dodgers and he wasn't really paying attention when he heard a resonant thud from the front of his vehicle. Then he was thinking what could have made that noise and it sounded like something was being dragged along the rear of his truck. He slammed on the brakes and saw a small dog run out from underneath. He thought maybe the sound was the dog and that the dog was OK, but deep down he knew something didn't add up when, from the other side of the street, he saw a young man carrying yellow flowers calling out and running into the street and he thought something pretty bad might have happened.

THE SPOONS OF JUPITER

And even those who fare reasonably well may carry with them inner wounds—a sense of emptiness and regret at having missed self-defining, confidence-inducing early experiences that cannot, in the final analysis, be recaptured.

—Laura E. Berk, *Awakening Children's Minds*

Author's Note: On 17 July 2018, the International Astronomical Union confirmed ten more moons around Jupiter, bringing the total number to seventy-nine.

Notecard #1

Good morning. As of today (insert date of presentation May _____, 1996), scientists have discovered 17 moons around Jupiter. There are probably more that haven't been detected yet.

The ones of most scientific interest are the Galilean satellites. These were the first objects found that didn't orbit either the Earth or the Sun. The other moons and the rings of Jupiter make up less than 1% of the total orbiting mass.

The moons are named after either lovers (hubba-hubba!) or daughters of the Roman God Jupiter or his Greek equivalent, Zeus.

I don't tell *her* how fat she is. Yet she needs to remind me every time I see her in the hallway to stop growing. I'm the Sears Tower, that's me. My sister's friend. Fat-ass Raquel. I ignored her and kept walking. The only problem was that I kept walking all the way down the hall, forgetting the whole reason I headed down Q-hall in the first place—to ask Cindy Butterfield to the prom.

So I broke my back and bent all the way down for a drink from the drinking fountain, all just as a pretense to turn around. I headed back up Q-hall, the way I had come. I could see down the hall; there was a bottleneck around a crowd of girls yapping away like a flock of squawking birds. So I inched around them with everybody else. I tend to blend in, even though I'm an ogre.

I nodded hello to this junior Jason Shinman, a real turd. He delivers pizzas at the same pizzeria I do and wears his hat brim so low that you can't even see his eyes. He barely even saw me, or maybe he pretended to barely see me. That's probably why he wears his hat so low—so he doesn't have to say hello to people he doesn't want to. A lot of that stuff goes on at my school. I kept creeping toward Cindy's locker.

All of a sudden, out of nowhere, my hands started sweating and my heart began thudding like mad, like it was trying to get out of my chest. So I stopped and pretended to be looking through my physics binder. A freshman girl walking behind me, about half my size, bumped smack into my ass. Her friends all laughed, because she bumped into a skyscraper.

I tried to laugh at how ridiculous the whole thing was: having to ask a girl I hardly know a week before the prom, a girl I've barely spoken to in four whole years of high school, a girl who has a boyfriend in college in Arizona who at the last minute decided he doesn't want to come all the way home to Chicago for a high school prom. She supposedly told her friends to tell my friends that I should ask her because she really wanted to go and already had a dress and we could go with the group as friends. They needed an extra couple to pay for the limo so all I had to do was ask her. Everyone was depending on me.

So there I was, frozen in Q-hall, getting in the way of everyone trying to get to class. I was like the scarecrow in *The Wonderful Wizard of Oz*. Not the movie, but the book by L. Frank Baum.

There's a part where Dorothy and her friends are on a raft, traveling to the Emerald City. The water gets real deep and it's hard for them to steer with the branches they're using as poles. So the scarecrow reaches way down and pushes real hard, only to get his pole stuck in the mud. Before he can pull it out, the raft is swept away beneath his feet. He's left clinging to his branch in the middle of the river. His friends are whisked away and he's left all alone, suspended over the rushing water. He starts wallowing in self-pity, lamenting his situation, because he's even more useless than when he was stuck to a pole in a cornfield. The best part is that the tin man can't even cry for him, because he'll rust.

And that's exactly how *I* felt, clinging to my science binder in the river Q-hall, stranded, with no one to cry for me.

I looked up at the clock and saw that I only had a minute before the second period bell. I snapped my binder shut and started walking. As I approached her locker, I caught a glimpse of her talking. She's an all right-looking girl. I mean she's no knockout, but she's not bad looking.

I couldn't believe it. Of all the people she could be talking to: Jessica Meddleson. Jessica is the best friend of a girl I used to see, Lizzy Silverthorne. Not that I ever even dated Lizzy. We were just friends for a while, until things got awkward. She has a boyfriend—some soccer player from another high school—and, truth is, I tried to kiss her once. I was really shit-faced at the time. I apologized like mad, but the damage was done. We had this tense phone conversation where no one really said anything.

Since then Jessica has regarded me like I have an elephant trunk instead of a nose. I could tell Jessica saw me out of the corner of her eye. I enjoy talking to her like I enjoy a good sinus infection. It would have to be after second period, I told myself, and glided right past them.

Notecard #2

The planet Jupiter's four largest moons are called the Galilean satellites after Italian astronomer Galileo Galilei, who first observed them in 1610. The German astronomer Simon Marius claimed to have seen the moons around the same time, but he did not publish his observations and so Galileo is given the credit for their discovery. Like Mr. Fair always says, your work doesn't count if you don't turn it in!

These large moons, named Io, Europa, Ganymede, and Callisto, are each distinctive worlds. They are nearly spherical in shape and are roughly the same size as Pluto, which, as you can tell from Jon Olson's presentation, would've been a much easier choice!

Side note: It's not good to be absent the day topics are chosen.

I had to run to get to physics too. "WAAALLLK!" some teacher yelled. Sure, and get a detention. No thanks. I made it just as the bell rang. Mr. Fair, my physics teacher, faked like he was going for the detention pad. Then he winked. I joke around with him quite a bit. He's got a real good sense of humor. Like when he's about to grade quizzes, I'll joke about how I'm going to invest in red pens. Something like that will really make him chuckle.

I sat down and Mr. Fair began to drone on about roller coasters. The class had recently gone on a field trip to an amusement park. I cut school that day, something I've been doing a lot lately.

Toward the end, Mr. Fair called out my name along with Jamie Kaven's—who's had mono and was sick for a month—because we were the only ones who hadn't done our presentations on any topic from outer space. Everyone else went like ten years ago. She hasn't gone because she's been sick, even after coming back to school. I almost did mine yesterday, but, if you really must know, I got stoned before school with my friend Hal. We were getting in his car on our way to school when suddenly I remembered the presentation. Hal thought it was hilarious that I had to get up in front of the class all baked.

"What's it on?" he asked.

And I accidentally said, "The spoons of Jupiter," instead of moons. That made Hal laugh even harder. He laughed the whole way to school and made me all paranoid.

"You're gonna say spoons, you're gonna say spoons, you're gonna say spoons," he taunted.

I ended up cutting that day as well. My grades were lousy anyway. The only leverage Mr. Fair had left is that I had to do my presentation to graduate.

There was only enough time for one and Mr. Fair asked who would like to go. He did it sarcastically, as if it would be a miracle for one of us to volunteer. Jamie said she wasn't ready and needed one more day to work on her visual aide. Her topic was the craters on the moon. I just sat there. My speech was all ready too. Finally Mr. Fair rolled his eyes and flipped a coin, and, sure enough, Jamie lost. She shot me a dirty look, then stood up and started babbling about how she forgot some poster and how she had an amazing visual aide that her uncle's friend from NASA sent her and it won't be as good without it but she *guessed* she would go today. Then, on her way up to the front of the class she did something that really gets under my skin. She told us, *before* her speech, how boring it was going to be.

I shouted out something witty as hell. I suggested that she could use her face as a visual aide. She had bad acne, all splotchy and red. I didn't even realize I was saying it. It just slipped out. I looked over and Mr. Fair was sending me to the Dean's office with an implacable face and pointing finger. I figured I could squirm out of it, but he wasn't budging.

"Tom Bedlam, to the Dean immediately," he said calmly. "And your presentation is tomorrow or you'll need a summer school registration form."

Notecard #3

Io is the most volcanically active body in the solar system. Io's surface is covered by sulfur in different colorful forms. As Io travels in its slightly elliptical orbit,

Jupiter's immense gravity causes "tides" in the solid surface that rise 300 feet (100 meters) high on Io, so better think twice about where you set that beach chair!

This generates enough heat for volcanic activity and drives off any water. Io's volcanoes are driven by hot silicate magma.

Io is a pretty big deal, as far as moons go. If you add up the mass of all the Jovian moons, Io accounts for 23%. So yeah.

I had to wait in the office for about five years. Finally, a robot that looked similar to Dean Early called me into his office and told me to have a seat. They played a recording through the ceiling while the robot's lips moved. I uttered the correct sound waves so that the robot signed a paper. Then the robot dismissed me with a stern monotone.

Notecard #4

Europa's surface is mostly water ice, and there is evidence that it may be covering an ocean of water or slushy ice beneath. Europa is thought to have twice as much water as does Earth. This moon intrigues astro-biologists because of its potential for having a "habit-able zone." Life forms have been found thriving near subterranean volcanoes on Earth and in other extreme locations (like Mr. Fair's classroom) that may be analo-gous to what may exist on Europa.

Europa has 12% of the total mass of Jovian moons.

I didn't get to trigonometry until halfway through third period. So I had missed my opportunity, because I usually saw Cindy in between second and third period in the hallway.

When I walked into trig class, both Keith Heffledorm and C.B. shot me these *did you ask her?* looks. They wanted a thumbs-up or a thumbs-down.

C.B. is a good friend of mine. Gosh, can he be a joker. He is always trying to make people laugh, and they usually do. Like on an elevator he'll start to whistle, "It's A Small World." It disarms most people, it really does. One time in study hall he just started meowing. Even the teacher was cracking up. So when I say he's funny, I mean like everyone-says-he's-going-to-be-famous-someday funny.

About six years ago, when C.B. was eleven years old, his dad died. For a while after that, C.B. didn't tell jokes or laugh or even smile. He even told me one time that he wanted to commit suicide. It really freaked me out. I kept my eye on him. He got through it all right. His dad had gotten pancreatic cancer and died in only a few months. Most people don't know that about C.B.—because they're always expecting him to make them laugh.

The reason I mention it is that the whole experience of losing his dad and getting through it has made C.B. sensitive about other people's feelings.

Most people don't notice, but there's never anyone at the butt of C.B.'s jokes. His humor is never at anyone's expense. It's just funny. Like when he opens a door, he'll smack the door with his hand and pretend that the door hit him in the face. He'll go all out and really do it up, like asking if his nose is bleeding. He'll do it out of the blue, just to tickle your funny bone. Or if it's windy he'll grab a street sign and hold himself up, so that he's parallel to the ground. "A little windy here!" It's pretty good.

Sometimes he does the door-in-the-nose joke so well—with perfect timing and a real loud SMACK—that if you didn't know him you'd think he was really hurt. One time Sara Katz, who isn't a brain surgeon, really thought he smashed his face. She was genuinely concerned. Sure enough, Keith Heffledorm and a few other vampires started laughing at Sara, but C.B. started using her sleeve to dab his nose so that Sara didn't feel bad. That's the kind of person C.B. is.

So he's at least a little sensitive about the whole prom thing. But he still gives me a hard time about it, too.

Then there's Keith Heffledorm. He's in my group of friends, yet I wouldn't say that he and I are friends beyond the circle. He can be pretty vicious. Like if you had a papercut, he'd be right there to squirt lemon juice on it if it could make another person laugh. Or one time I got a little too drunk and made out with this girl Meredith Lee, who has a fake tooth from when she knocked it out as a kid. She'll always pull out her tooth and goof around, except she's done it about three hundred times too many. So Keith will say, "Hey, how was it making out with Meredith's tooth?" There's always someone at the butt of his jokes.

When I walked in and saw their looks, I played like I didn't understand. They didn't go for it, though. I tried to mouth that I didn't have a chance to ask her. Hopefully they'll never lose their hearing, because they can't read lips to save their lives. Finally Ms. Crawford, my trig teacher, stepped in, asking us if we had something to share. Keith thought it over, lacking only a flash of fangs.

She went back to blathering about equations. The lights were off and the overhead projector was on. I started brooding about prom, like it's the apex of human experience. Every day at lunch the discussions are the same: blowjobs and tuxedos and limos and bedrooms. I try to laugh and go along with it, but inside I'm squirming.

Suddenly, Ms. Crawford called on me to answer a problem. Of course, I didn't even know which question we were on. The silence hung up in the air for a moment.

Luckily, the bell rang, letting me off the hook.

Notecard #5

Close-up images taken by the Galileo spacecraft of portions of Europa's surface show places where ice has broken up and moved apart, and where liquid may have come from below and frozen smoothly on the surface. The low number of craters on Europa leads scientists to believe that a subsurface ocean has been present in recent geologic history and may still exist today. The heat needed to melt the ice in a place so far from the Sun is thought to come from inside Europa, resulting primarily from the same type of tidal forces that drive Io's volcanoes.

Still, you better bring a microwave if you want to heat up some pizza!

C.B. and Keith worked me over a little for not asking her after first period. I assured them, I would do it. They had nothing to worry about.

"When?" C.B. wanted to know.

"After lunch."

I headed to gym and left it at that.

In gym we were supposed to go outside for softball, but it was raining so Coach Marsh just gave out basketballs and let people shoot around. He was my freshman basketball coach. He called me a noodle once and it has always stayed with me.

"You're like a wet noodle, Tommy Lamb, just a floppy wet noodle," he said with his hands on my shoulders, shaking me.

Not that anyone else even remembers. Yet *I* do—three years later. And I probably always will. I can still hear his chirpy voice as he grabbed me by the shoulders and shook me.

Of course he didn't put it together that my mom was sick and we were eating a lot of frozen dinners and things like that, but still, I always resented him after that.

I was cut the next year. People are always asking me if I play basketball because I'm so tall, and it really depresses me. It's just one more thing orbiting my head.

I got into a three-on-three game. When Coach Marsh called, "Balls in!" the game was tied. Well, two of the guys in the game, Irakli and Leo, have the biggest rivalry in all of basketball going, save Bird and Magic. Irakli is from a little country in Eastern Europe called Georgia, and Leo is Russian—so it gets pretty intense. We played next bucket wins, but no one could score. The game went on and on, and still no one made a shot. Even Coach Marsh came over and tried to get the ball, but just then Irakli hit a jumper. Leo was furious. He thought Irakli had traveled. He started calling Irakli, "Broccoli," which is really a way to push his buttons.

We had already given back our gym lockers since it was the end of the year. So we played in our regular clothes. I was dripping. I even had sweat stains beneath my armpits.

We were the last ones leaving the gym. Sure enough, who comes around the corner but Cindy. The only thing that surprised me is that I didn't have a nosebleed or maybe a black eye. Leo and Irakli were still arguing at the top of their lungs.

She came around the corner unexpectedly. I almost didn't even say hello to her.

Notecard #6

Ganymede is the largest moon in the solar system (larger than the planet Mercury), and is the only moon known to have its own internally generated magnetic field. It makes up roughly 38% of the mass of Jovian moons.

Callisto's surface is heavily cratered and ancient—a visible record of events from the early history of the solar system. However, the very few small craters on Callisto indicate a small degree of current surface activity. (Like possibly Bigfoot's vacation home.) Callisto has 27% of the mass of Jovian moons. It is a stereotypical outer solar system satellite. So don't feel bad if people are stereotyping you; it happens to moons too.

I got to English class a little early and asked Mr. White if I could go to the bathroom. "Is it an emergency?" he asked. What a question. I was dripping in sweat.

"Be back before class starts," he said.

What a humanitarian. Sorry I didn't zip my fly—there was no time!

I walked in about five minutes late. Mr. White gave me a tardy, which is a tenth of a point off your grade average, but I had a solid D in his class.

My problem in Mr. White's class began when I started writing papers sans punctuation. I guess I just got tired of writing what teachers wanted to read. You know: introduction, body, conclusion—blahblahblahblahblah A+. Splendid paper, you wrote exactly what we told you to write. So I started turning in some James Joyce soliloquy papers. Mr. White wasn't exactly impressed with my precociousness.

I started to get all annoyed, but I decided to tune him out. I was in the back so I read my book, *The Sound and the Fury*. I had just started it and was having trouble following the first section. All I can really tell you is that Caddy smelled like trees.

Notecard #7

The interiors of Io, Europa and Ganymede have a layered structure (as does Earth). Io has a core and a mantle of at least partially molten rock, topped by a crust of solid rock coated with sulfur compounds. Europa and Ganymede both have a core; a rock envelope around the core; a thick, soft ice layer; and a thin crust of impure water ice. In the case of Europa, a global subsurface water layer probably lies just below the icy crust. Layering on Callisto is less well defined and appears to be mainly a mixture of ice and rock.

It's like one of Mr. Fair's stories—full of layers with obscure meanings.

I didn't hear much of the conversation during lunch. I was thinking about when I would ask Cindy. She didn't have the same lunch period, but there would be ample opportunity that afternoon. They had planned a whole slew of senior activities. At least classes were cancelled. Everyone else was talking about tuxedos and blowjobs again. The best night of your life.

When I got up to throw away my lunch, I just kept walking, all the way to the library. The bell rang and everyone headed outside for the class picture. The seniors gather in this spot where they've done the senior class picture for the last forty years and then the principal comes out on the roof and snaps the picture. They hang the picture in the main hall where you become another dot on the wall.

After the third "Caddy smelled like trees" I slammed *The Sound and the Fury* shut, which made the librarian jump. I wasn't about to sit in that library all afternoon. By the time I got out for the picture, though, everyone was heading in.

I didn't bother looking for Cindy. The truth is, I sort of hid behind a tree and let everyone pass by.

It had stopped raining. I stood looking at all the footprints and puddles. I don't know what trees smell like, but it smelled good, fresh, from the rain.

Notecard #8

Three of the moons influence each other in an interesting way. Io is in a tug-of-war with Ganymede and Europa, and Europa's orbital period (time to go around Jupiter once) is twice Io's period, and Ganymede's period is twice that of Europa. In other words, every time Ganymede goes around Jupiter once, Europa makes two orbits and Io makes four orbits. The moons all keep the same face toward Jupiter as they orbit, meaning that each moon turns once on its axis for every orbit around Jupiter. This is called synchronous motion, which is like our moon and why you never see the dark side of the moon unless you're watching The Wizard of Oz while listening to Pink Floyd.

It's all enough to make your head spin!

The next senior activity was to dip your hand in paint and put a handprint on the wall of the senior cafeteria, where it stays for one year until the next class paints over the wall and does the same thing. I figured I would leave as little evidence of myself as possible. For a moment I started getting that frozen-in-the-river feeling, just standing around, towering over people. C.B. was pretending he didn't know that he had paint on his hand, walking around and trying to get people to shake hands with him. He was really hamming it up.

"Hey, Josh, great year, great year! We gotta hang out this summer."

Josh Taustein extended his hand, unaware that everyone was watching. But C.B. pulled his hand away at the last moment. Keith started doing it, but he *would* shake the person's hand. He went up to Gary Shickman with everyone watching.

"Gaaaaarrrrr!" Keith said. "Great year, buddy!"

Old Shickadoo took the bait hook, line, and sinker. He turned red as a stop sign as everyone laughed.

"You got me. Good one," he said.

He'll probably carry that rotten moment around the rest of his life.

C.B. went over and did it to Dean Early. C.B. pulled his hand away, but Dean Early, being the dork he is, actually wanted to shake with C.B. after the joke, to show how he was a good guy and all. So C.B. smeared paint on his hand. I wanted to puke.

It was almost time for the assembly. They do a mock party and then an accident with a mock funeral with all the teachers as actors, then the county coroner comes in and tells us not to drink and drive because she doesn't want to knock on our parents' door at 3 a.m. People were heading to the bathrooms to wash their hands on their way toward the auditorium.

"Hey, did you do a handprint?"

It was C.B.

"No. I didn't feel like it."

"Dude, what's up with that?"

"With what?"

"With the whole C-Creepio act? You know, creepin' out. Not doing a handprint. Not going to prom. Not being in the picture. You're missing out on everything."

C-Creepio. Whenever anything was slightly creepy, it was C-Creepio, like C-3PO from *Star Wars*.

"I'm just not up for it."

"Laaaammmme." He started sounding an alarm, like it was a "lame alert."

"Listen," he said. "I just saw Cindy at the class picture. She asked me if you're going to ask her. All you gotta do is ask. OK? You can do it, ain't no thang. Better than sitting at home eating a bowl of Honey Nut Creepios."

I put some green paint on my hand and did an eight-finger print, without writing my name. C.B. did a pirate hook, but he wanted his name beside it.

Notecard #9

Pioneer 10 and 11 (1973 to 1974) and Voyager 1 and 2 (1979) offered striking color views and global perspectives from their flybys of the Jupiter system. Starting in 1995, the Galileo spacecraft made observations from repeated elliptical orbits around Jupiter, passing as low as 162 miles (261 kilometers) over the surfaces of the Galilean moons. These close approaches resulted in images with unprecedented detail of selected portions of the surfaces. (Indicate the poster here.) You know you're in outer space when 162 miles is considered extremely close!

The biggest discoveries from Galileo are probably the crisscrossed cracks on the icy surface of Europa, suggesting the possibility of running water or even an ocean. Also, the large red spot on Jupiter is not a religious symbol to ward off bad luck—it's actually a huge hurricane with counterclockwise winds of over 250 miles per hour!

A math teacher named Mrs. Wagner, wearing all black for her role in the assembly, came around the corner.

"Boys, you're going to miss the start of the assembly."

We washed our hands and ran to the assembly just as they were dimming the lights. We walked down the aisle. I couldn't see anything. I slowed down, trying to see if there were any seats. It was packed. Then Vanessa Welter and Becky Sorenstein waved at us. They're both pretty good-looking, even if they are a little snobby. C.B. is real good with the ladies, using his sense of humor and all. He went right over and sat down, pretending to accidentally sit on their laps first. They started giggling. There was only one open seat, so I kept walking. I had walked all the way to the front row and now didn't have a seat. Of course I was blocking people's view of Dean Early's introduction—a real captivating orator. Right behind me was Glen Smith, another humanitarian, who calls me "Lurch" from the *The Addams Family.* Sure enough, he called out, "Lurch, down in front."

I stood there awkwardly with that frozen feeling. A lot of people were laughing. Then Dean Early snapped me out of it. He paused from his profound address to say something else that will always stay with me.

I was on the verge of something really pathetic, like crying or telling everyone what I really thought of them, when out of nowhere an arm reached out and saved me. Sure enough, good old Mr. Fair grabbed me by the shoulder and pulled me down into his seat. He winked at me and then headed over to lean against the wall.

I drifted back out into an orbit, floating around with all the things that were spinning in my head. I kept hearing Dean Early telling the senior class, "Tom Bedlam, you're going to be late for your own funeral."

Once it was over, I did my vanishing act again. I was near the exit, so I slipped out after they turned the lights on. I headed straight to the parking lot. I have a 1978 Buick LeSabre. It's shit-brown. For a while I used to drive quite a bit on the weekends, going out with everyone while they drank. You can bet I had a lot of friends. But then Will Boone, the starting QB, threw up in the backseat. Go ahead and guess who ended up cleaning it. I'll give you a hint: It wasn't Boone. I stopped being everyone's chauffeur after that. I can still smell the puke, mingled with pizza.

In the parking lot I paused and almost turned around and went back. Maybe I could still find Cindy. I was about to, when someone called my name.

Of all people, Jason Shinman and his hat. He came running up.

"Damn, man, you gotta work the afternoon shift? You really bolted outta there. Can't wait to leave this hellhole?" He laughed a plastic laugh.

I didn't say anything.

"It's a good thing you're so tall. I could see you amongst the cars."

I almost punched him right in the brim.

"Anyway, man, are you going to prom?"

"I don't know yet."

"Well, I wasn't going to go, since it's so expensive—but then this afternoon outta nowhere this girl asked *me*."

I don't even know why I asked.

"Cindy Butterfield. I guess she has a college boyfriend or something that screwed her over at the last minute. You could say I'm doing her a favor. She already has the tickets so I don't even have to pay. I'm pretty psyched."

"Congratulations."

"Yeah, well, thanks, but there's one problem."

"Oh yeah, what's that?"

"Well, I'm supposed to be delivering pizzas that night."

"Bummer."

"Do you think you could cover my shift, if you decide not to go? It should be a big money night."

"I'll let you know."

He said something else, but I just walked away. I had to. I didn't want him to see me cry.

Notecard #10

As you can see from my visual aide, the numerous Jovian moons exhibit an astonishing variety of features. Many are captured asteroids that have changed little in the past 4.5 billion years, but others have shown extensive signs of past, recent, or ongoing activity. So if you get captured next time you play capture the flag, don't despair; at least you won't be held for billions of years!

I got in my pizza-puke-smelling shit-brown Buick and drove off. I didn't look back. I went right through a red light, like the whole world was one stupid traffic light. I gunned it through another yellow and was lucky I didn't get into an accident, out in space thinking about what it would be like delivering pizzas to prom parties. I drove even faster and before I knew it I was almost at my house when I realized I had to go to the shrink, the one I've been going to since my mom died.

I burned rubber over to his office and took the stairs up. When I got to the office, though, there was a young guy with a beard standing next to my shrink.

"This is Jared," Dr. Hilgenberg said. "He's my new associate, and I thought you might try talking to him this afternoon."

"Sure, whatever," I said.

"It's nice to meet you," Jared said.

We shook hands. I noticed he had the word "breathe" tattooed on his thumb.

"There's a garden in back of the building." Jared said. "Why don't we go there?"

"Sure, whatever," I said again.

"Follow me." He led me out of the office.

We went down the stairs and out a back door, then followed this gravel path around the building and back through some trees where there was a small opening with plants and a little fountain and a bunch of different stacks of balanced rocks.

"Have a seat," he said, indicating a bench. We sat down and he started.

"The most important thing I can do for you today is listen," he said. "To make you feel heard and, hopefully, understood."

I nodded and stared at a stack of rocks.

"Is there anything upsetting you? Anything you want to share?"

I was quiet for a little, listening to the trickle of the fountain. Finally, I said, "What's the point? I never get anywhere talking about it. It just goes round and round."

"Try me."

I took a deep breath and told him about it. The whole sordid drama starting back at Q-hall.

When I was finally done, he went over and picked up a large rock with a big jagged point.

"Is it fair to say that the experience you just shared with me is like the side of this rock? Sharp? Painful to touch?"

"Sure."

"Let's say this rock represents the memory you will have of not going to prom, and that not only do you have to carry it your whole life, but you will have to build on it in forming intimate relationships."

He set the rock down with the sharp point up.

"Would you agree that it would be hard to stack another rock on this? To try to build anything or reach another level?"

"I'm no gravity expert, but sure."

"What would it take, then, to make this large, jagged rock different, to change it so it is more like this one over here? Smaller. Flat. Smooth. Easy to build on."

"A jack hammer?"

"True, that would work," he said, laughing. "But I left my jackhammer up in the office."

He paused for me to say something; when I looked away he started again.

"I think that's a good starting point for next week. You mentioned Faulkner and Joyce. Well, I would like you to try to write about this experience, maybe put it into a story. Use your sense of humor. As you write it, or maybe when you're finished, see if you can view this experience differently, as something that can be a foundation for understanding."

He held out his hand.

"And please bring it in," he said as we shook. "I would like to read it."

I got in my car. For the first time since I started going to a shrink, I actually didn't feel worse when I left. I got home and there was a message from C.B. on the answering machine.

"Hey Creeps, heard Butterfield asked Shinman. That's what you get for screwing around all day. But give me a call. I think we might still have a date for you. Hal's girlfriend has a friend from Lowland Park. Call me."

When he said Hal, that's when I remembered that I had to do a presentation tomorrow, senior ditch day, the last day of school, on—of all things—the moons of Jupiter.

Notecard #11

In conclusion, together we can take a bird's-eye view of Jupiter and its moons. I know there aren't birds in outer space, but just go with it. Looking down (indicate poster), we see in the center the awesome gas giant Jupiter, the fifth planet from the Sun, with a mass two-and-a-half times that of all the other planets in the solar system combined.

Orbiting relatively close to the planet are the four large Galilean moons that orbit in prograde motion, or the same direction as Jupiter's rotation. (Indicate and show motion.) Farther out are two smaller moons that also orbit in prograde motion. Then, as we get farther away, we see a tangled mess of smaller moons that orbit in retrograde motion, or the opposite direction of Jupiter.

It is possible and even likely that someday there will be a collision amongst Jupiter's outer moons. Especially if they find a moon amongst the retrograde that orbits with prograde motion, this could be quite a spectacular astronomical event—even greater than the time Mr. Fair bumped into Paul Deagan!

That's all, folks! The information in this report comes from NASA and my encyclopedia at home. Are there any questions?

PHUC'S GARAGE: A HISTORY

History is an organic process, a continuity of related events, inexorable yet not inevitable.

> —Stanley Karnow

We bought the last available house in the second phase of a new development in the North County of San Diego called Luminara Hills. We got a good deal because they were anxious to start selling the third and final phase. It was just dumb luck.

We moved in on the first of October. Festival Street, like life itself carried the promise of an endless party. Wendy was newly pregnant. Harrison was two.

The neighborhood sloped to the west, towards the ocean, which on clear days we could just see, peeking between green hills, a deep blue line on the horizon. Everyone was very nice. There were lots of families with young kids. To the east was the third phase: an empty street with new, vacant houses curling up around a hill, then sloping down to a cul-de-sac.

In the evenings I would take Harrison out on walks. He was learning to ride a scooter. All the action was to the west, with kids running everywhere, shouting, lost in imaginary worlds, darting in and out of garages, riding all types of wheels: bikes, rollerblades, skateboards, etc. … But it was too much for

Harrison. So we went east, uphill along the empty houses, around the bend and then down a hill and into the cul-de-sac with a large bluff of rocks jutting out, looming above. It was peaceful. There wasn't any development on the hills above. Sometimes, late at night, we heard packs of coyotes yelping in the vast darkness.

Harrison and I never saw anyone on our walks, except every once in a while there'd be an old Asian man, ambling stiffly, like he had been riding a horse too long. I think he had some kind of hip ailment. Sometimes he would wave, but we never talked to him and I never did see which house he came out of. He always just appeared, like from behind one of the recently planted trees, out of thin air.

On the return trip we always had one stop: the mailbox at the bend. One night our next-door neighbor Lyla was there, and I asked her about the old guy.

She frowned like I was describing a six-legged coyote, but then a smile of intrigue broke through her clenched lips.

"Maybe it's a ghost?"

I gave Harrison my best *she's only kidding* smile and thought back to when Wendy and I met Lyla. Not long after hand-delivering homemade oatmeal raisin cookies, she had whispered her theory that an older, single neighbor named Carol was dead in the house two doors down.

"It's been weeks since anyone's seen her," she had said with an ominous turn of her head. "I bet she's just lying in there, dead, waiting to be discovered." Carol came back a week later from her European cruise.

"Who knew?" Lyla said the next time we all met at the mailbox. She had shrugged and told us a joke. "If you're Russian in the kitchen and Asian in the living room, what are you in the bathroom? You're-a-peein'!"

Towards the end of the month, we saw Lyla at the mailbox again.

"By the way, I still haven't seen your ghost," she said, glancing up from her envelopes and junk mail.

"We haven't seen him in a little while, either," I replied. "Maybe he'll be out on Halloween?"

"Maybe, with all the other ghosts. By the way, did you hear about Beth and Ted?"

She shifted to a hushed tone and used her mail to cover her lips, like someone might be trying to read them. It was a few nights ago. A big row in the middle of the night from the house on the corner. It woke half the street.

"I only see Ted now," she added. "Never Beth. And he never stops to chat."

I offered another vague shrug.

She leaned in and whispered, "I bet he hacked her to pieces."

I took our mail and nodded like it was within the realm possibility. Harrison was on the nearby slope, investigating snails. "C'mon buddy, it's getting dark."

A few days later a For Sale sign appeared on the corner and word spread: Ted and Beth were freshly divorced.

That October was a hot month, for both weather and the housing market. Young families snatched up the new houses like hotcakes. When November hit, the weather and the market both finally started to cool. Thanksgiving was approaching and it was getting darker for our walks to the cul-de-sac. It had been a full month since we last spotted the old man.

Harrison was feeling more confident on his scooter.

"I ride myself?" he asked from under his giant spiderman helmet.

"Let me go with you," I said.

"No." His favorite word. "Just me."

"All right. Just go down and back," I said. "So I can see you."

I followed along behind him as the road curved, then watched him ride down the hill, skidding his shoes along the pavement the whole way, down to where the houses were not quite finished. Right before he reached the cul-de-sac, I saw him slow down and look at something. He turned and scurried back up the hill, like something was wrong. When he came back he was out of breath and puzzled.

"Daddy, there's a man sleeping on the sidewalk."

"What?"

He pointed. "Down there. A man sleeping."

I couldn't see anything. "Go back home," I said. "Go in the house and find Mommy." As soon as he disappeared into our house, I trotted down and, sure enough, right near the mouth of the dead end along a big boulder that bulged out, the old Asian man was lying face down. I ran over and turned him onto his back. His forehead was bleeding. He was thin and had a scraggly gray goatee. I noticed a single black ant crawling down his cheek like a tear.

I felt his pulse. He was still breathing. I dialed 911 and glanced at all the new, modern houses with empty windows and closed doors. Then I started CPR. A fire station was just on the other side of the hill, so I knew it wouldn't be long.

I kept up the pumps to his chest and puffs of air as the siren grew from faint to loud. His lips felt like rubber and his breath reeked like rotten vegetables. The ambulance arrived in minutes.

As the paramedics put him on a stretcher and affixed an oxygen mask to his face, I asked them if they had any way of finding out the man's identity.

"We know him," one medic said. "He lives in that old house tucked back behind the rocks. Has forever. It used to be the only thing out here."

I looked over toward the bluff and didn't see any house.

"What house?"

"Exactly," the medic said.

The ambulance pulled away and I walked back past the empty windows of sold houses that hadn't been moved into yet. I half expected someone to duck down or a curtain to sweep closed. When I got back, Wendy was cooking dinner and Harrison was playing with LEGOs.

"What was that all about?" she asked.

"Did you know that there's an old house back behind the rocks beyond the cul-de-sac that's not part of the development?"

"Really?"

"Well, that old Asian guy lives there and he was lying unconscious in the street," I said. I glanced at Harrison. "An ambulance came and took him away. I think he might D-I-E."

The next night Harrison insisted I go with him. I walked to the end of the cul-de-sac. The curb flattened out and there was a little opening in front of a gate that led to an access road to a water reservoir on the other side of the hill. I walked up to the opening and, sure enough, snaking off to the side was a little gravel trail, just wide enough for a car, twisting off back behind the rocks. I walked up a ways and saw, way back behind the bluff, a long, thin, S-shaped structure surrounded by trees.

"Daddy? … Daddy? Where are you?"

"Here. I'm here."

I didn't realize at the time that I wasn't looking at a house. Only the garage.

*

"Tell me absolutely everything," Lyla said at the mailbox. So I did.

"I had no idea there was a house back there," she said with dinner-plate eyes. We stood there looking at each other at sunset, wondering what other surprises lurked in Luminara Hills. Buried treasures? An ancient city?

As it turned out, he didn't D-I-E. In early December we were out on our walk in the gathering darkness.

"Daddy! The man that was sleeping," Harrison said. "He woke up!"

The man paused from his plodding and waved.

"Good evening," I said from across the street. "Are you feeling better?"

He smiled and nodded, lifting his feet like they were concrete blocks to cross the street. He trudged over and gave Harrison a cookie wrapped in plastic. He mumbled, something like, "Ban Dan Xan," and lumbered right along.

"Can I eat it, Daddy?" Harrison asked once he had moved on.

"Sure; don't tell your mom."

He took a tentative bite.

"I don't like it," he said. "It's spicy."

It was almost Christmas when we saw him again. All the houses had new families, decorations on the bare plots, and signs for the landscape companies redesigning the front yards.

He shuffled out from behind a worker's truck parked on the street and said with a heavy accent and an overemphasis on the last word, "Did you enjoy *cookie*?"

Harrison buried his face in my legs and I said, "Yes. Very much."

He nodded and moved on. That was the last time we saw him.

"I bet he's just lying in that house, D-E-A-D, waiting for someone to find him," Lyla said as the new calendar flipped to February. "We should go up there. Check it out."

But no one ever did.

Then it was the Fourth of July and we had a new baby girl. I remember it was pushing a hundred degrees. For the first time in its young history, Festival Street's east and west sides got together for a big party. The kids had just finished a big bicycle parade when around the corner lumbered a large U-Haul.

"Who moves in on the Fourth of July?" said John, a west side neighbor I had just met. He had been telling me about his business selling handcrafted knives.

Once the street was clear, a young Asian family smiled and waved from the truck's cab like they were part of the parade. Behind them came an SUV, crammed full of boxes, another Asian man driving. The two vehicles drove on through the cul-de-sac, right up to the gate that leads to the reservoir access road, then turned up the gravel path toward the old house.

"The pocketknife," John said. "That's your bestseller right there."

All that day the SUV came through the celebration, the family inside smiling and waving like they didn't know that the parade was long over. It would leave empty and come back full of boxes. The last time it came through, they interrupted a fireworks show courtesy of Amanda, another new west side neighbor, that had just moved from Colorado.

"Maybe the ghost of the old man is still up there," Lyla said as a bottle rocket exploded. "About to haunt the living shit out of this nice, clueless family."

By August, Harrison was fearless on his scooter and joined in with the kids in the cul-de-sac. We started going out after dinner. We would take the baby sleeping in the stroller and stay out until dusk. One warm evening I was talking with Amanda about the Broncos. Heat pulsed from the pavement. Out of the long shadows of the rocks, the young family emerged from the gravel path. I recognized the father as the driver of the U-Haul. His wife walked alongside, carrying a baby and holding the hand of a young girl wearing a *Doc McStuffins* T-shirt.

I gave them a *howdy, neighbor!* sort of wave. They strolled up to us, all smiles, short, well-dressed, polite.

Phuc introduced himself with a wide, bright smile.

"Like Luke," he said. "But with a *ffff* sound. It's spelled P-H-U-C. It's Vietnamese." He had a faint accent.

He seemed to have way more teeth than me. His wife introduced herself as Bian. She held a baby boy named Than.

Phuc told me that his son was eleven months old. They had just moved down from the Bay Area. He was a branch manager at a local Bank of America.

"Welcome to the neighborhood," Amanda said. "And what's your name?" she asked, addressing the young girl, who promptly hid behind her father's legs.

"Tell them your name," Phuc said.

Harrison arrived on his scooter.

"I bet you can tell us *your* name," Phuc said to him.

He barely whispered his name, but Phuc heard it.

"Harrison! That's a beautiful name. This is Kim!" he said, indicating the small girl wrapped around his leg. "Say hi, Kim!"

Kim waved.

"How old are you Harrison?" Phuc asked.

Harrison held up three fingers.

"Three! Oh my goodness! Kim is three also!"

The two toddlers regarded each other and seemed to weigh the validity of this information. Harrison was much taller. He lingered another moment and then scooted off.

Bian looked down at the baby sleeping. "What a beautiful child!" she said. "What's her name?"

"Everett," I said. "We call her Evie."

"So cute."

A silence hung in the air, so I filled it. "We were wondering what happened to the older gentleman that lived here. We used to see him walking."

"That was my father," he said. "Now he lives in an assisted living facility in Carlsbad. When I was transferred, it just made sense for us to move into the house and for him to have his own space. It's so hard to find housing."

"Oh," I said. "A lot of people were wondering if he was OK."

"Yes, he's fine. He's fine. He was a homeowner here long before the development. We'll have people up to see the house once it's in order."

Amanda also worked at a bank, and the conversation drifted in that direction. We chatted for a little while longer before they left.

"Nice meeting you too," I said, using my *howdy, neighbor!* wave again.

Later, I was telling Wendy about Phuc and his name.

She spelled it back to me. "P-H-U-C? Like fook?" she said. "You've got to be kidding."

"For Phuc's sake, I wouldn't fookin' kid you about Phuc!"

She gave me a *very funny* smile and then said, "Well, Lord knows our neighborhood could use a little diversity."

*

The next week, while our kids were riding scooters in the street, Phuc set me straight about his name. He laughed about it and said it comes up all the time. But even as he joked, he was very proud of his name.

"In Vietnam, names carry a powerful force," he said. I'm six-two and he only came up to my chest. He looked up at me without a trace of inferiority. "My name means luck, blessings. Which is true—I have lived the American dream. My family moved to the United States in the '50s to escape the war with the French. I grew up in Dallas. I love the Cowboys!" He lifted his shirt sleeve to reveal the Cowboys star logo tattooed on his shoulder.

Amanda and John drifted over. Phuc told us how his old branch manager in San Francisco would always tell the employees, "Don't fook with Phuc!"

We talked football for a while but then his daughter skinned her knee. When the kids were scooting again, the subject returned to Vietnamese names.

"In my culture names have a lot of meaning," Phuc said, smiling but somehow very serious. "My daughter's name Kim means gold. Than means delicate sky. Tradition claims that evil spirits like to steal babies, particularly attractive ones. In the countryside, where old customs linger longer, new parents go to great lengths to make their children seem unappealing. They would never compliment their newborns. Instead, they call them 'ugly' or 'rat' or even 'shit' in order to trick the spirits into staying away."

John took the opportunity to announce that his wife was pregnant. They weren't going to find out the gender this time so he and his wife had just started discussing potential names.

"I won't be offended if you call him or her a shitty rat," John joked.

"In that case, may you have the ugliest piece of shit rat baby," Phuc joked back with a beaming smile. Phuc was always smiling. I liked him.

As I was walking home, I thought about his life and how different it was from mine—growing up in San Diego, surfing and playing soccer. Then something he said echoed in my mind. "The war with the French."

"What war with the French?" I thought to myself. I'm not exactly a history buff. So you can't blame me that nothing occurred to me a few months later, when I was just getting to really know Phuc, the night he told me all about the history of his garage.

*

"Why don't you stop by tonight, after the kids are in bed, and we can have a drink or two out back?" he had said as I sauntered over from the mailbox.

"Sure, I always need a drink about then," I said, nodding at Harrison swinging a stick in an imaginary battle.

I went over a couple hours later. I walked up the gravel path that wound through boulders. I felt like a kid again, discovering a secret trail in the woods behind Stagecoach Park. After a few switchbacks, I came to the steps leading up to his house, shrouded with trees. It was like a cave or a grotto, tucked into the earth. At the top of the steps, a presence in the darkness startled me so that I almost fell backward. I found myself face-to-face with a large statue that I learned later was a water buffalo. I patted it on its head. "Stay. Good boy."

All I could see of the house was a structure that followed the rocky slope and curved in a long, thin S shape. The architecture was unusual. Without knowing much about it, I'd say it looked like an ancient eastern temple. It had a sweeping timber roof with the corners curling toward the sky. Tiers were stacked above it diminutively like a pagoda. Wooden posts with arches lined the adobe walls as part of the framework. Despite the curves, the structure had a symmetry that was aesthetically pleasing. It was quite beautiful.

Maybe the color was another reason I hadn't noticed it on any of our walks. The walls were the same orangish-brown as the granite hillside. The tiered roofs were the exact green of the chaparral bushes. Looking closer through the trees, I noticed a small thread of yellow running along the border between the walls and the roof.

I walked towards the S-shaped structure when I heard voices behind the main house. I followed a lighted path that took me around the house and to Phuc's backyard.

A few other west side dads were there; I had met them a handful of times but couldn't quite remember their names. Phuc handed me a beer.

"You guys know Bruce?" Phuc said.

"Sure," they said.

I mentioned that I thought the S structure was his house, that I didn't realize how much land was back here. He had an impressive backyard. Gas fire pit. Pool. Hot tub. Barbeque. Pergola.

"Yes," Phuc smiled. "That's the garage."

I thought he was going to say more, but one of the guys asked him about the tiles on the patio. Everything was brand new. None of this was here before. His father was a man of "simple means." I looked over at the garage and thought about this.

At the end of the night we all exchanged numbers. I started to get texts inviting me once or twice a week. It became a regular thing. I would head over with a couple beers and relax for an hour or so. Phuc's backyard became like the neighborhood saloon for dads that needed a break in the action. It felt very exclusive and private. We used to call them Phuc'n breaks.

The night he told me about the garage though, it was just him and me.

*

On this night, a Friday, after I finished my two beers, Phuc offered me an iced drink in a giant bowl of a glass. It was some Vietnamese cocktail. Something with bourbon and ginger.

"Try it, you'll like it." Phuc winked.

We sat with the cocktails by his fire pit. The blue flames flickered, and the shiny glass stones of the fire pit illuminated Phuc's face. Still, even in the darkness, his teeth were gleaming. He wore a Cowboys hat with a big blue and white star.

"If you'd be willing to hear it," he said, "I would like to share with you a story."

"Sure," I said, taking a small sip of my cocktail. It was strong but had a sweetness that helped it go down. "I like a good tale as much as the next guy."

"Well," he said, "It's a true story, the history of my garage. But it's really the history of my family. And like all good historians, I will start as far back as I can. Back before there was ever a Luminara Hills."

He paused to take a drink, and I had the feeling that he was about to confess something to me.

"For a long time there were just a few homes that dotted these chaparral hills. During this period, there were no HOAs, or Homeowners Associations, which now have come to domi-nate most developments in the North County of San Diego, including our own Luminara Hills community. Which is why my garage is so much bigger than everyone else's," he said with his wide smile.

I came to learn that Phuc's grandfather was the original owner of the house, and his father, the old man I used to see walking stiffly, grew up in the house. This is when the original conflict of the garage began.

"My grandfather's childhood friend Han needed a place to store a motorcycle he was repairing," Phuc said, sipping his own fishbowl of a drink. "And so he kept it there, and then started bringing in boxes and other storage. He just thought he could, since the motorcycle was already there, and since they had been friends all their lives.

"But my grandfather's sister, named Trung, refused to let Han just take over the garage. He was now storing a good deal of stuff there. Trung had four kids and she wanted to store stuff too, like baby clothes and a crib. She argued the garage should be only for family members. It came to blows one night and she threw all Han's stuff out onto the street—it was just a dirt road then," Phuc said, pointing over his shoulder toward the street below. His teeth and eyes reflected the light from the fire pit. There were a few lights on in the yard; the night sky was full of stars.

"My grandfather smoothed it out and there was this long period where my grandfather, his friend Han, and his sister Trung shared the garage in harmony. But it all came to an end when another sister, Ding, found out about the arrangement and wanted to store her kids' bicycles. There was an extended period of strife between the two sisters over the remaining space. They would steal each other's stuff, sell it, or just throw it away. By this time my grandfather was older and had grown weary of the whole affair.

"Then my grandmother passed away," Phuc said. "My grandfather was grieving, and the garage was the last thing on his mind." He took a drink, as if in remembrance. I joined him.

"I always think," Phuc paused, and for the first time since I had known him he looked a little sad, "that if she had lived, none of this would have happened." He took another drink, a long one at that. My bowl was half full, and it was going straight to my head.

"Well, it was around this time that they developed Luminara Hills Road. When the road was developed, it literally paved the way for more housing. So my grandfather got two new neighbors, one on each hillside: Cam Bickerson and Fran Charles.

"Fran was a minister," Phuc explained, indicating with his bowl toward a large house on an opposing hillside that apparently used to belong to Fran. "He ran this big church out in East County, but then he lost the church. I don't know… maybe he couldn't make rent or something. So he needed a place to store all the stuff.

"During this time my father, Ho, went away to college to become a doctor. He studied all over the world. He did his undergraduate in New York, then medical school in Paris, with his rotations taking him to Russia, Germany, and China. After graduating, he worked for Doctors Without Borders and served in many places: South America, Africa, even our home country Vietnam. Finally, he decided to return here to start his own practice, which he ran for thirty years before retiring, probably a few years before you moved in."

I nodded. "Could be. We moved in last October."

"I'm ready for another," he said, standing. "You've got some catching up to do. Drink. It's Friday."

Phuc darted over to his bar. I finished my bowl, chewed on some ice, and looked up at the stars. He walked back briskly with two more bowls, like he was eager to prevent both my throat and the story from going dry. I set my empty bowl down by the fire and we touched glasses as he sat down across from me.

"So while he was gone my grandfather's sister Ding's husband, Duc, allowed Fran to move all his church storage into the garage, to the great annoyance of everyone else—the other sister Trung, Han. Even my grandfather, according to my dad, wasn't happy with the arrangement. Are you following? There are a lot of characters with monosyllabic names," he said and laughed.

"So when my dad came back from all his travels, he apparently gathered up the whole family: Trung, Ding, all of their offspring and relatives, nieces and nephews and cousins, along with my grandfather's friend Han and Han's son—an impressive gathering." Phuc used his drink to indicate, as if all of them were sitting with us that night, around the fire. "After some debate, Ho allowed my grandfather to invite Fran as well."

Then he added, with special emphasis, "If it was up to my father, Fran would never have been at that meeting." He paused for a moment and removed his Cowboys cap, feeling the edges of the star. I was tired. Part of me was like, Why should I give a rip about this garage? But the other part of me noticed Phuc's earnestness and said, Pay attention. This garage means something. Then he resumed.

"That night, before the meeting, the family agreed on a sacred pact, that nothing would stop them from getting full and independent control of the garage. At that point Ding and Duc and Trung had this argument about how all the family garages and storage spaces should be shared and used collectively. (All the other relatives lived in apartments, so the storage was really important to them.) Ho, surprised at the vehemence of the argument, sat and listened as Gia, Trung's daughter, argued persuasively for a common system that could benefit all. Meanwhile Ding faced pressure from his son, Bodey, to keep his own garage free and independent, with Bodey arguing there should be a democratic process every couple years to determine who gets what space based on actual need, which was all a bold-faced lie— he just wanted it for himself because he figured he could control the elections. The argument lasted long into the night, until finally Ho stood and declared, 'The use of this garage and how it will be divided is unsettled. What is clear is that the garage belongs to the family, no matter how we choose to divide it.'

"Apparently it was a very tense moment, with everyone relieved but also looking at Han and Fran, thinking, 'He's talking about you guys. You're not family. Why don't you get out of our garage?'"

"Well," Phuc said, pausing as the flames of his fire pit surged, like a connection existed between the story and his gas line. "It was right around this time that the development in the area exploded. Suddenly homes lined the entire hillside and, like night following day, in California an HOA follows development.

"Ho was back in Paris and didn't even know that my grandfather's house was being entered into the HOA. He came home furious that we weren't, pardon the pun, grandfathered out of the HOA.

"So Ho was livid and the HOA wasn't too happy with Ho having a garage twice the size of all the other garages in the development. Never mind the architecture or that you can't see it from the street. There were all kinds of HOA codes that it called into question. Ho relied on Han's son Moe, a lawyer, and also another lawyer named Sergei he knew that lived in Carlsbad, to fight them off. Also, the HOA was well aware of Fran's church pews and clutter being stored there. But not everyone on the board was aware that Fran was a friend of the first HOA administration and the HOA president. His name was Marshall Murtan. They were trying to create this code that allowed Fran to store *his* stuff there, but not people from outside the association."

"All of this over a garage?" I said incredulously, swirling my drink.

"Right?" And he continued, talking even faster. "Well, the HOA fire got hotter, and old Han and all his descendants said, 'We're out. We don't want anything to do with this whole HOA business.' But secretly they really wanted Trung and Ding and all their descendants like Gia and Bodey to keep fighting the HOA, to weaken it so they could have their sway in neighboring communities. Fran, tired of fighting with the sisters, in a mostly symbolic gesture moved his stuff from the South end of the garage to the North, since Han left this space open. So Fran said, in effect, 'I'll move, but I won't get out.'"

Phuc took a small sip. I was having a hard time keeping up, both with the story and the alcohol consumption.

"It was a big mess, with Fran refusing to pull out his church boxes and pews, Duc and Gia and now Bodey fighting over the southern storage space and also about how best to get rid of Fran, and the HOA on the sidelines meddling with the whole affair because they couldn't have a garage that didn't line up with their codes, yet also supporting Fran's right to store his church stuff. And you've got Cam, the other neighbor, and his son, Sean, right next door, just trying to stay neutral.

"Apparently, my dad says that this guy Marshall was worried that if Han took control of our garage and allowed it to be a common system of sharing, then all the neighbors would protest and they would want their garages to have the same sharing capabilities, too, and that it would be like one big game of dominoes: all the garages, then all the yards, and then all the houses, free of the HOA and each living communally."

Phuc just shook his head and laughed, sensing correctly that I needed a moment to absorb all the information about the various factions and conflicts. When I nodded, he proceeded, slower now, but only a little, like the story was rolling down one of the dark hills around us and he was powerless to slow it down.

"So Han and his son Moe started having success, legal victories, in neighborhoods in nearby Escondido, so that all the garages there could be used in common and storage can come from outside the neighborhoods. Then the same thing happened over in Vista, with neighborhoods complaining about the small garages in certain developments and deciding to share the garages as a whole.

"Well, you can imagine Murtan—"

"Who?" I said. I was halfway through the second cocktail and things were getting blurry. The second drink tasted even stronger.

"Marshall Murtan, the HOA president," Phuc said, laughing. "C'mon, that's an American name."

"Oh, right."

"So Murtan was getting his panties in a bunch. He got involved in this Vista fight, taking them to court, saying you can't have the garages shared in common, that it violates these principles of Home Ownership. So here's what Murtan did: He sent in ants. Can you believe it? The HOAs had this tactic that if things weren't going their way in communities, they would drop ant colonies all around the homes in the offending area. Of course the homeowners just fought back with pesticides and other ant-removal techniques, with countless ants getting slaughtered, quite needlessly, but that's what these leaders decided.

"Ants?"

"Ants," he said, nodding. "In fact, that was the one thing my father regrets most from this whole ordeal. The loss of life. He believes, deep in his heart, that all life is sacred. He has dementia now. Believe it or not, he has several ant farms in his room. He loves to watch them work. The colonies. He finds it so interesting. I just brought him another one the other day. He now has four in his little room. The nurses all call him the Ant Man."

"The Ant Man?" I said, shaking my head.

"Yup," Phuc said, flashing a smile, leaning back, drinking. But when he leaned forward, the smile was gone and he was all business again.

"So Murtan sent the ants into Vista. Meanwhile Han was having more success in Escondido, growing more powerful, all while supporting, along with Sergei, the effort to get Fran out. His son had like a full takeover of the garages in all of Escondido. The entire town started sharing their garages. You can imagine Murtan not being too happy about that, either. But, his term as HOA president was over.

"The new HOA president was named Isaac Howard, but everyone just called him Eyes. Well, Eyes was a pretty shrewd guy and he settled the whole Vista thing, stopped planting ants furtively in people's homes and all that.

Phuc saw the question forming on my face.

"No one really knows how old Eyes did it, but he did it just the same. The big event that happened next was that Fran and Gia played a game of chess: Winner would get half the garage and loser would get nothing, squat. The old boot. Well Fran thought that he had some kind of moral and legal right to the garage, that he had been there so long, that God needed the space, and that my grandfather benefitted from the whole arrangement somehow. Also, Fran greatly underestimated Gia's ability in chess. She had been playing and studying for years, right under Fran's nose, but he just figured he could walk in and get an easy win. Not so. Gia wiped the floor with him. Destroyed him. An embarrassment. And the whole time Eyes and Fran's attorney and the HOA were in talks about the garage, with this sinking feeling that all the talk was a moot point because Fran had to get his stuff cleared out ASAP."

"A game of chess?" I asked.

"Amazing, right? Playing chess for garage space. I couldn't make this stuff up."

"Fact is often stranger than fiction," I assented.

"You might be thinking, Why do these facts even matter?" Phuc said, his eyes gleaming a little. "And I would ask you back, Why does *any* history matter?"

He took my silence as his cue.

"So Gia took over the North of the garage and Bodey took up the South. And then the old stalemate reared its ugly head again. Gia wanted the garage to be a common use for all the family members, just as my father wanted it, and the way—if she was still alive—my grandmother would have had it if my grandfather didn't give it away in the first place in what became known as, The Original Blunder. Bodey was for free, independent garages with a cycle of elections based on need, which might have worked if it wasn't obviously corrupt and didn't kowtow to the HOA and their regulations."

"So there's a battle of belief systems about how the garage should be used?"

"Exactly," Phuc said, moving his bowl toward me with such enthusiasm that I noticed some spilled into the fire pit, sizzling in the blue flames. "So Bodey, recognizing that Gia had the upper hand, in a classic Vietnamese face-saving move appointed his brother, Tim, who also happened to be on good terms with Eyes, as the leader of the South garage, so that the stalemate really settled and hardened: Tim and a free system vs. Gia and a common system."

Phuc put his drink down and his smile went away. He removed his cap and scratched his short jet-black hair. He put the hat down on his knee, and the smile returned as wide as ever.

"Even though it's just a garage," he said, "it's a tale as old as the stars: the clash of ideas." And with that he looked up at the stars. I gazed too. It was a beautiful night and I couldn't help but think of how all this unfolded underneath the same stars, like silent witnesses.

Phuc resumed. "The HOA was helping out Tim and trying to pass codes and regulations to have free, independent garages that follow HOA regulations, while old Sergei, Ho's friend and lawyer in Carlsbad, was secretly pushing for common garages. And the fight continued all through Eye's term."

He put his hat back on and took a sip from his bowl, which was almost empty.

"Time passed with no progress, and Eyes was out of office. The next HOA president was this young guy, Jules Ferdinand Klingenhoffenmeyer. Well, his name was so long that everyone called him JFK, just like your fallen president," and Phuc polished off his last bit in a big gulp, like he was drinking for the assassinated leader.

"And then JFK got involved in another garage incident, down in Mission Bay, because this guy Delfi had this whole guinea pig operation and was storing the pigs—from Russia of all places—in people's garages. But it all blew up in JFK's face because what would an HOA president of a community in Luminara Hills be doing meddling in an entirely separate HOA community in Mission Bay? The whole thing gave JFK a real black eye and is still known in HOA circles as the Bay of Guinea Pigs fiasco."

"The Bay of Guinea Pigs?" I said, shaking my head.

"You got it. Another nod to your president," Phuc said. "You would think that the guinea pigs would have been enough for JFK to steer clear of Mission Bay entirely, but another incident came along. It was revealed that my father's lawyer friend Sergei and his group of Carlsbad lawyers wanted to store these Cuban muscle boats in Mission Bay garages. Again JFK puts his nose where it didn't belong, at least to a lot of onlookers, but he ended up getting the muscle boats out of Mission Bay in what HOA circles call the Cuban Muscle Boat Crisis."

"The Cuban *Muscle Boat* Crisis?"

"One more? Whaddya say? We're not working tomorrow, right?"

Again Phuc dashed off to his bar. I took a long drink, and then another, and finally one more to finish off my bowl. He was back again with what I felt was a sense of urgency.

"To our families," he said, holding up his glass. "And their futures." Our glasses clinked, and as I sipped what had to be the strongest drink yet, he dove back in.

"In the meantime, things weren't going so well back in my grandfather's garage. My grandfather, fed up with the squabbling and incessant bickering between Gia and Tim, ended up painting it orange. All the residents of the communities below called it the Orange Suicide, because it was such a bright, loud orange marring an otherwise pristine hillside, and no matter how many coats of paint, you would never be able to completely cover it.

"JFK and the HOA were deeply troubled by the Orange Suicide, but before he could do anything, JFK abruptly left office. Maybe it was the Bay of Guinea Pigs or the Cuban Muscle Boat Crisis. The story has it that right next door to the HOA office is a 7-Eleven, and that JFK favored Slurpees. One day he drank a big slurp, had horrible brain freeze, and up and quit right on the spot. Like his brain just froze and he couldn't take it. Reports are buried away in HOA files, but the theory is that a lone madman tampered with his Slurpee, like made it extra cold or something. JFK's brain freeze is a matter of legend now, and is still debated within HOA circles of San Diego. Many think it was a conspiracy. Some contend it was the Cubans seeking revenge over the muscle boats. Others think it was the Russians still seething over the guinea pigs. The evidence points to it being a lone 7-Eleven employee that opposed the free, independent system of HOA garage storage. Brain freeze or not, JFK was out as president."

"JFK's brain froze," I said, not really sure if it was a statement or a question.

"Right. His replacement—who wasn't elected, mind you—also had an absurdly long name: Lionel Bartholomew Jorgenson. So he just went by LBJ."

"So wait," I said. "LBJ replaced JFK as HOA president."

"Right."

"And you're not making this up. This really happened."

"It's all in the HOA history books," Phuc said. "Look it up. The repetition of history is, sometimes…" and he paused, looking into the fire, for the first time since he began the story he was at a loss for words. He stared for a time, the Cowboy star covering his face, and then he looked up at me, right in the eye, and said, "Quite exquisite."

Then it was my turn to be at a loss for words. Phuc took up the reins again.

"Around the same time, coincidentally, Tim disappeared. He either up and moved or did something wild, because he vanished from the scene. Some say he joined the Coast Guard. Anyway, his cousin Kevin stepped in and took control of the southern part of the garage—he had the same policies and outlook—and he called it a free garage of the people. As far as the HOA was concerned, all of the descendants of Ding were the same: inept, inefficient, and corruptible.

"By this time, the HOA was fed up with the whole garage struggle and just wanted LBJ to fix it. They gave him a Tonkin Truck for his desk that symbolically represented extraordinary powers never before bestowed upon an HOA president. Sure enough, LBJ started sending in the ants to my grandfather's garage. So began another long, drawn out, and sordid affair. The HOA kept increasing the ants, but in the meantime Gia had managed to carve a secret trail running from the back of the garage to Cam's house. They called it the HoCam Trail. From there Cam smuggled all these secret ant repellants and traps, paid for by Sergei and Moe. The HOA found out about the trail, so it ordered something never before issued in HOA warfare: stink bombs."

"They started bombing the HoCam Trail?" I asked.

"They went bananas," Phuc said, gulping his drink. "The HOA started bombing the trail, the garage, and even the countryside and surrounding neighborhoods with full-on, rotten-egg stink bombs. All the residents began protesting to the HOA, but it didn't stop the bombing. For a miserable period of nine years, the HOA kept up the ant and bombing campaign.

"The campaign proved to be very unpopular amongst residents. Countless dead ants covered the roads and sidewalks, needlessly slaughtered." Phuc took his longest drink yet. I took another drink and looked at him across the fire. His eyes glistened and for a moment I thought I was sitting with a person that had slipped into madness.

"And the thing is, this LBJ character, he had some really good ideas for improving the neighborhoods. But not *one of them* did he accomplish. Instead, the battle over my grandfather's garage marred his entire term in office.

"During this period, both Sergei in Carlsbad and Moe in Escondido would continue to help out Gia. They would give her supplies and money and all kinds of things to deal with the bombings and the ants. Most effective of all, though, was that Gia and Ho developed their own ants, red fire ants that they colonized along the HoCam Trail. They were fierce, loyal, and willing to endure unimaginable hardships, including the bombings. The red fire ants suffered great casualties, but as Ho famously proclaimed, 'You can kill ten of my ants for every one of yours, and I still win.'"

Phuc finished his drink and poured the ice onto the fire, watching it fizzle. He took off his hat and tossed it onto a table.

"It was a very tumultuous time in Luminara Hills history. Other houses painted orange squares as a demonstration. Residents were protesting the HOA's bombing. The HOA itself capitulated to the demonstrations and reduced the ant invasions, which were largely misguided and ineffective—much like Fran's chess strategy.

"Then a real turning point took place. See, Ho was by this time estranged from Kevin and Ding's entire branch of the family tree. He saw them as traitors and puppets for the HOA. He believed they would turn all the garages into free, independent garages that weren't actually free, as he put it, but just stooges to the HOA. So he coordinated with Gia what became known as the Tot Offensive."

"Tot? Like tater tot?"

"Yes, like tater tot," he said, thrown for a moment.

"Because I'm getting kind of hung—"

Phuc waved his hand at me. "They turned the North end of the garage into a daycare center and filled it with toddlers. Tots. Slowly and gradually, the Tots infiltrated the South. The toys, the noise, the diapers, it simply overwhelmed Kevin and the HOA trying to help him to keep a tenuous grasp on the South so that garages would remain free to the families and owners, and not subject to common garage networks.

"There were actually negotiations between Ho and Gia and the HOA during this period, but they never went anywhere. To think, what was it all for? All those ants, all that needless money spent on stink bombs, life and time and resources. It all could have been saved, if both sides weren't so concerned about the old Asian custom of Saving Face. But that's not how my father or Gia or their side saw it; they stood by their principles and their decisions. Either way, the HOA wouldn't halt their bombing campaign, and the North wouldn't give up their positions in the South, so it was another stalemate.

"When LBJ finished JFK's term, he decided not to run for reelection. I guess he saw the writing on the wall. His garage policies were so unpopular that it appeared he didn't have a chance, especially with JFK's brother RFK gaining traction as a candidate, pledging to end the War on Garages."

"RFK?" I asked. I was close to spinning, with the fire and Phuc and the stars and the story, so that I had a hard time keeping my full drink from spilling. But still, I remember that one registering.

"Right," Phuc said. "Reuben Ferdinand Klingenhoffenmeyer. RFK. But wouldn't you know it, RFK had a Slurpee accident too. Some lunatic at the 7-Eleven hit him with a Slurpee point-blank and just like that, he decided he didn't want all the flak that came with being an HOA president and quit. Just like his brother, RFK—only a candidate—had his HOA service tragically cut short."

Phuc's eyes were like two small balls of fire. The night wasn't cold, but I got a chill down my back.

"So into the void stepped in this other candidate, a man who had lost to JFK years earlier, Dick Noxin. The whole time Noxin kept up LBJ's failed HOA policies, though he tried to appear that he wasn't. He kept reducing the ants, but increasing the stink bombs. He had his top assistant, Mr. Kiss, as he was known, meeting in secret with a member of Gia's side: Duke.

But it all went nowhere—just more ants and bombs and fighting over the garage.

"One night there was this big, horrible crash of Mai Tai glasses, really special glasses that had been in the family for generations. No one knew how they broke, but everyone suspected the HOA. It's known in my family as the Mai Tai Massacre.

"Noxin even began to bomb Cam's house, in secret. Meanwhile Mr. Kiss was meeting with Sergei and Duke in swanky Carlsbad restaurants. And Noxin himself even took this big trip to Escondido to meet with Moe—the symbolic leader of the common garage movement. All the while, though, Noxin stepped up the stink bombs directly on the North half of the garage.

"The residents, meanwhile, kept up the protests. Four residents got stung by bees believed to be planted by the HOA in a house owned by Kent Stadler, known as the Kent Stadler Stingings. But Noxin didn't care and was sort of a master at controlling the message. He managed to convince many residents that the bombing was necessary or else all HOA's everywhere would fall apart and this wave of common garages would take over neighborhoods from La Jolla to San Bernardino.

"It could've continued like that for longer—bombs and ants and the struggle over storage ideologies—but some plumbers working in the HOA office found out that Noxin was clogging pipes with some intestinal condition that he later lied about. I guess he used to eat 7-Eleven hot dogs all the time, which he also denied. Tapes of him buying multiple chili cheese dogs proved that he lied, so he had to resign.

"The next HOA president, Jerry Chevy, about as All-American as it gets, listened to the residents and shut down the war on my grandfather's garage. No more ants. No more bombs. It was over. And without the HOA's support, Kevin had to surrender. The toddlers just overtook him. There was a brief period when Kevin acted as if he could hold his own ground, but he had no chance against all those two- and three-year-olds. They don't call them the Terrible Two's for nothing. You and I know that."

I was quiet for a while and Phuc smiled at me. He turned off the gas to the fire; it was mostly just starlight now. I really had to pee. Phuc sensed I was about to get up and he leaned forward, very close to my face.

"You would think that would be the end of it." He leaned even closer. I could smell the bourbon. "But this morning, Moe's son Kurt put a box in my garage."

My bladder screamed. I put down my full bowl of booze and said, "Great story. I'm going to head home."

He shook my hand and I left. He sat back down though. I looked back at him sitting in the darkness. I was drunk, stumbling, and had to steady myself against the water buffalo.

*

It was five or six years later when the PBS documentary about the Vietnam War aired, so I caught an episode. I still went over to Phuc's for a beer from time to time, but it was rather infrequent. One night I mentioned the series.

"Fascinating. Horrible and astounding," he said.

I DVRed the series and watched it over the next few weeks.

"Vietnam, again?" Wendy would say, grabbing a magazine.

When the credits rolled on the last episode, I realized I still wanted to know more. So next time I was at the library I picked up Stanley Karnow's 670-page *Vietnam: A History, The First Complete Account of Vietnam at War.*

I'm not really a reader. Mostly I read news here and there on the internet and gossip in *People* magazine. I'll listen to a book on tape, if I'm on a road trip. But I've never really been able to sit down and read a book—especially one as long as Karnow's. But I got into it. I guess you could say I just wanted to understand the whole thing, the whole mess. As a son of a veteran and an American, I felt reading it was something akin to civic duty.

Maybe I'm not a reader because I'm so slow. I'm slower than slow. I had to renew the book and still only reached the Geneva Convention of 1954 on page 204. Then someone put a hold on it. Probably also inspired by the PBS special. I got busy and sort of forgot. But the need to understand, that never went away.

So another couple of years passed. I was at the library with my kids and thought about the book. It was in, so I checked it out. This time I really set aside some time and studied it. I had to go back and reread the beginning. The first chapter, "The War Nobody Won," is a Big Picture, "the foundering American century on the shoals of Vietnam" kind of introduction. Then chapter two, "Piety and Power," goes way back, before the French, into ancient Vietnamese history. It was fascinating stuff. I was hooked, reading it every night before bed.

"How's your book?" Wendy would ask, the way you might ask someone eating plain noodles how their meal is.

"Very interesting, *thankyouverymuch*," I would say back, and she would roll her eyes.

With starting over, and my slow, plodding reading, I still only got to the Tet Offensive on page 530 when my three renewals were up. So then I had to return it *again* and, wouldn't you know it someone got it before I could check it back out.

"Why don't you just buy it?" my neighbor John asked. "It's probably like five bucks on Amazon."

"Yeah, I don't know," I said. "It's the principle of it. Why pay for something I can read for free?"

John shook his head and walked away. "You and your principles. And I need my wheelbarrow back."

I put a hold order on the book and checked it out one more time. Then it hit me, all at once—that whole night with Phuc. I remember I was on page 652, reading about Nixon's new operation, Linebacker Two, an eleven-day bombing campaign (excluding Christmas) over the heavily populated corridor that stretched between Hanoi and Haiphong. Just like the forty thousand tons of bombs slowly falling, so did the realization descend in my mind that the history of Vietnam bore a striking resemblance to the history of Phuc's garage.

I started to tell my wife about it, but she wasn't interested.

"For Phuc's sake—turn off the light and go to bed. It's after eleven."

A week later, Bank of America transferred Phuc and he moved his family to Seattle. A new family moved into his house. Word on the street is that they're from Bangladesh. They mostly stay to themselves. I'm not on social media or anything, so Phuc and I have lost touch. Sometimes I think of that night, of the whole saga about his garage, and wonder if any of it really happened.

A HERO, TO GO

She's always losing her keys. She's never on time. It's always someone else's fault. But it never bothers her in the slightest. It's aggravating, is what it is. Watching her stroll into the café behind sunglasses as if the whole notion of time and units of time that pass consistently and steadily onward is less important than that her shoes match or that her nails are perfect.

She sits down and takes off her sunglasses.

"You'll never believe how far I had to walk to get here," she says.

"There are things I'll never believe, all right," I say back, but she cuts me off. All about the cabbie's B.O. She couldn't stand it.

"But weren't you sitting?" I say, and it's like I never even said anything.

"It ought to be a law for cab drivers to shower," she says, grabbing a menu. "And this menu is *filthy*." Because of one smudge.

I dip my napkin in water, and it's like I'm offering her dirty toilet paper. I extend another menu, and it's like I'm a sex offender.

"I don't see why we had to meet here," she says, wiping the menu with her napkin. "You know I don't care for Italian for lunch. It's so heavy." She looks at the menu like it's a mortuary pamphlet.

I take a sip of iced tea and chew a cube. I crunch it down and chew another. The ice feels good between my teeth. "There are specials," I say finally.

"These specials aren't all that special," she says. "What's special about lasagna?"

"They have salads," I offer.

The waiter comes by. She orders bottled water at room temperature, a glass, no ice, with lemon on a plate. Absolutely no tap water. Never tap water.

"I'll have her ice," I say. "And another glass of iced tea."

"Coming right up," the waiter says.

"He's about Jack's age, don't you think?"

"I don't know. Maybe," I say. This is my ex-wife. And this is our lunch, once a month, *for the sake of the children*. Always for the sake of the children. The sake. Of. The Children. THE SAKE. The children's sake. The sake sake sake.

This is what I do. I say things over and over again until they lose their meaning. This is not for the sake of the children. This is for her sake. Just like the water. I am that water. Our marriage was that water. The temperature was never right. It needed this or that. Why can't you just do it? For the sake of the children. Always.

We sit in silence. I watch people arrive for the lunch rush. The restaurant is filling up. It always does. The best Italian in the Bronx. She rummages through her purse and pulls out her new toy: a mobile phone.

"You should get one," she says. "It's practical. It could save your life."

"How's a phone going to save my life?"

She frowns and pushes some buttons. "I think Barbara called me while I was walking," she says. So I repeat my question.

"Oh I don't know. If you have a stroke or something." She tosses the phone back in her purse like I've just asked the Dumbest Question In The History Of The World.

The waiter comes by with the drinks. He pours the water and stands back, like it's wine and she has to approve the temperature. Which she does. My ex.

"Are you ready to order?" he asks.

"Oh no. I couldn't possibly," she says.

"I can come back," he says and walks away. She takes a big sip and swishes it around.

First, she's late, and now she can't order. I have one hour for this. Then it's back to work I go. But she doesn't care. She has all day to sit around and do nothing but cash the checks I send her.

"Do you think our waiter is gay?"

"What?"

"I think he might be gay," she says. "He looks to be about Jack's age. I don't see a ring. He appears to be fit. Maybe we should ask if he's single?"

"Or if he rides an elephant to work," I think but don't say. My ex. That's her new thing. She never accepted our son's homosexuality. Fifteen, sixteen years of denial until last month, when she became his matchmaker.

"What makes you think—oh, never mind."

"Fine," she says. "Be that way. You're always that way."

I don't say anything. It's better when I don't say anything.

"I simply don't have a clue what I should order," she says. "Everything looks so heavy. Even the soup. Maybe I can just get broth."

A busboy comes by, cradling a basket of bread, with a pitcher of ice water in one hand and a bin of dishes under his other arm. He's sweating. I watch as he almost makes the fatal decision to pour ice water in her glass. He drops a basket of bread and then gets the ninth degree about whether the bread is gluten-free. It's obvious he doesn't speak English and has no idea what celiac disease is.

"Do you know if it's baked on the premises?" she asks.

"There's rye," he says.

As my ex interrogates him, a tall man in a suit with silver hair comes in. He has a big entourage, all in suits, and the crowded restaurant buzzes a little bit, like it's somebody famous. I can't see his face. My ex finally releases the busboy, sending him on an errand to ask the kitchen if they have gluten-free crackers, and he bumps smack into one of the suits. He drops his tub of dishes and there's a big crash. One of the suits is splattered with tomato sauce. The entourage moves around the melee and I never do see Silver Hair's face. They sit down in the corner booth right behind my ex as her phone rings with a loud, obnoxious tone.

"Hello, Barbara," she says.

Barbara. The best friend. Martyrs of Divorce. They start in, and I see the waiter on his way. I look at my watch and figure I may as well order for myself. My future son-in-law has to work his way around the busboy cleaning up the broken dishes, and, what with the noisy restaurant, he doesn't hear me call out for a hero sandwich. He goes right on by and starts to take drink orders for the table with the suits.

The manager comes over to placate the splattered suit.

"I don't think the bill is gonna cover the dry cleaning," the man says in a thick Italian accent. I listen to the manager apologize some more and I almost miss my future son-in-law passing by again.

"A hero," I say. "Can I get a hero, please?" But he's gone. I think one of the other suits slipped him some cash. I may as well put in an order for dinner.

I start twiddling my thumbs, watching the minutes go by. Great, so I won't even get to eat. Not even for the children's sake. I look at the back of Silver Hair's head. It looks like he's fresh from the barbershop.

Then a small man in a red cap comes up to the table of suits. He removes his cap and appears to be a little nervous. I would be too. They look like mob guys, right out of a movie. The restaurant starts buzzing, like electricity is flowing through the place, with people pointing and staring.

I try to listen in, with my ex asking Barbara all about how her maid is doing this and that and a hundred other pointless problems.

"I'd like to introduce myself," the man in the red cap says. My ex keeps uttering, "You poor thing." Still, I catch his name. Simon Garfunk. Then my ex finally closes her yap hole.

"I'm a songwriter," Simon Garfunk says. "I've heard a rumor that you were upset with one of my songs."

There's a tense moment, like one of the suits might put a slug in him. The whole restaurant is watching, listening, frozen. Except my ex.

"Sure, sure, I've heard of it," Silver Hair says. He has a broad, muscular back. I'm thinking he's some kind of actor. "Please, have a seat," he says. "Vinny."

The man with the soiled suit stands up. I guess he's Vinny. He makes room for Simon Garfunk. I'm racking my brain. The name is very familiar but I don't know American music that well. Did he sing "Sweet Caroline"? Maybe if I wasn't half-starved I could think. Meanwhile the Martyrs have moved on to their favorite subject: the faults of their ex-husbands. My ex calls the restaurant a godforsaken place.

The waiter walks by with a bottle of wine and a tray full of glasses. I can feel it, the electricity. It's in the air. Everyone is excited. I move over to sit next to my ex to try and listen in. Well, you can guess how that goes over. You'd think I wasn't wearing pants by her reaction.

"Take it easy," I say, scooting down and turning my body. Real casual. The waiter is filling glasses for the table of suits. Silver Hair asks Simon Garfunk to have a glass. The waiter walks by, fast, like he's got to get the glass right away or Vinny's gonna pop him, so he doesn't hear my call for a hero sandwich, even though I practically shout it this time. I bet Barbara heard me.

"What I don't understand," says Silver Hair, "is why you ask in the song where I've gone? I just did a Mr. Coffee commercial, I'm a spokesman for the Bowery Savings Bank, and I haven't gone anywhere."

I see the waiter coming back with a glass for Simon Garfunk. I hold up my finger, trying to get my future son-in-law's attention, but he buzzes right by me. "I just need a hero," I say. "I'm late for work."

But he walks right by me to deliver the glass. Simon says thank you and starts to speak.

"I didn't mean the line literally," he tells Silver Hair. "Songwriting is all about syllables. Your name just fit."

My ex hangs up with Barbara and starts barking at me to move back to my side. "Just a second," I say, but she keeps nagging. Vinny does his best to give the table privacy. Everyone is looking, and a man tries to come over and take a picture. But Vinny doesn't let him. I'm trying to hear what the singer is saying, to figure out who Silver Hair is, trying to get my future son-in-law's attention, who's busy talking to one of the suits about an appetizer, and all the while absorbing the incessant nagging that will be the death of me. I can't make out a word.

Finally, I give up on the whole thing and go back to my side of the table. Simon Garfunk stands up and shakes hands with Silver Hair. I can read their lips. They say goodbye to each other.

"Call me Joe," Silver Hair says.

The restaurant is full of gasps and faces that all look like they've seen a ghost, like Silver Hair is some kind of angel down from heaven.

I start chewing an ice cube, and my ex lays into me for my disgusting habit. Finally our future son-in-law comes over.

"Are you ready to order?" he says.

"Does your minestrone have barley?" my ex asks.

"If it's not too much trouble," I say, "I'll take a hero to go."

THE ISLANDS OF SOUTHERN CALIFORNIA

"Good morning, class! Today we'll be learning about a unique ecosystem that's just to the north of us: the Channel Islands off the coast. We will begin by watching a video and then doing a short reading. For the video, please write down a minimum of ten things you learned. Everybody ready? Here we go."

*

"They come and go," he said. "They are like the wind."

"Well," she said. "I'll do what you think is best."

"I don't know what to do."

"We can go to the ER if you think we should."

"I don't want to deal with all that."

"If you think it's necessary, we should go. Better safe than sorry."

"What makes me think I should is that I have been off aspirin for over ten days," he said. "And the risk of irregular heartbeats if your blood isn't thinned is a stroke. The clot travels to the brain."

"Why don't you take an aspirin now?" she asked.

"Yeah, maybe I should."

"What do your papers say? How long should you wait after it before you can take aspirin again?"

"It says ten days prior and three days after."

"So, isn't this the third day? Why don't you take one?"

"OK."

She got out of bed and went over to the medicine cabinet in the bathroom. She tossed him the bottle, and he swallowed a small yellow pill.

He laid back, closed his eyes, and felt his pulse. "It's not a-fib. Just palpitations."

"Mmm-hmm."

"Damn unsettling though. Like missing a beat and then a really strong one. They come and go like the wind."

"I'll do whatever you want. If you want to go to the ER, I can call my sister and she can watch the kids."

"I just want to sleep."

They were quiet for a time. She was reading, and he was lying with his eyes closed and feeling the pulse of his carotid artery along his neck.

"Well, at least I don't have to worry about it as another trigger."

"Huh?"

"You know, like coffee, vigorous exercise and cold water have been the triggers for my other a-fib episodes. But it's not like I'm going to have my balls snipped again."

*

1. An archipelago is a chain, or cluster of islands. The Channel Islands form an eight-island archipelago along the Santa Barbara Channel in the Pacific Ocean off the coast of Southern California. Human remains have been

discovered there from as early as 13,000 years ago. The islands are home to 150 unique species of plants found nowhere else in the world.

I have no time for writing, is what he always said and truthfully believed. Every time I sit down I'm exhausted and write shit. And then I never come back to the shit to try to clean it up. It's just all shit. Sitting in a Google drive. A giant pile of digital excrement.

There'll be time, she said, like T.S. Eliot he thought, remembering how he had been carrying a volume of Eliot's selected poems the night they met—as if this was evidence that could be used. There will be time. We have the rest of our lives, she said. We only have this time to have children. You can write full-time once the kids are in school and I'll go to work. But then it will be too late, he thought, much later.

He was about to doze off, finally, but then a strong beat woke him and he was wide awake. He looked out the three windows at the night sky. There were stars and a planet. Certainly it has to be a planet. It's too bright to be a star, he thought. His heart beat erratically and uncomfortably in his chest. Lub-dub… lub dub… DUBDUBDUB… lub… dublub… Lub-dub… Lub-dub…

Eight years. That is how long we have been in this house, he thought. For eight years I have been watching the sky through these three windows. It has gone so quickly. Days. Weeks. Months. Years. Dawns and sunsets and darkness and light. Storms and clear skies. All through these three windows.

His heart seemed to stop beating for a full breath before it burst forward with a string of beats. DUBDUBDUB

Now it seemed death would come through one of the windows. But which one? It was like the game they played on the scoreboard at the Bulls games during a timeout. His father had taken him to Chicago Stadium to see the great Michael Jordan Bulls. They were tickets given to his father, the education guru, by a political friend who would come too, so he had to wear a white collared shirt under his red sweatshirt. First row balcony. He could still see the scoreboard with the giant Bull, the Budweiser, Gatorade, Coca-Cola, and Winston signs, the players numbers and points along the side: 23, 5, 33, 54, 24. He was looking out the windows but seeing the scoreboard at the old Chicago Stadium: There were three cups but only one had the ball. They showed you the ball and then rearranged the cups very quickly. If you really concentrated you could follow it.

And now it was like that. He was concentrating, his heart beating unsteadily along, looking at the window with the planet, the one with the stars, and the clear one, and trying to figure out which one death would come through.

*

2. Chumash society flourished for thousands of years. Spaniards arrived in 1542 led by Juan Rodriguez Cabrillo.

3. A tragic meeting of European and Native cultures, smallpox and measles forced the Chumash from their island homes into missions by the 1800's.

He had wasted his twenties. After college he spent six dreary months in his Chicago suburban childhood home, waiting tables and tuning out the advice of his father to become a teacher.

He wrote one story: a blatant Kafkaesque rip-off called "An Orbit" inspired by Kafka's "Description of a Struggle." He had read Kafka's work and tried to imitate it, but the imitation came off poorly. Whenever he wanted to rework it, he would look in the libraries and bookstores for "Description of a Struggle" but could never find it, like the spark that had started the whole story was gone and couldn't be recaptured. Once he wondered if such a story existed or if maybe he imagined it, until he looked it up on the internet. But he didn't order the story. It was something other than laziness and more like avoidance.

He showed "An Orbit" to his friend Farley, who liked it and graded it like an English professor, writing in comments and suggestions on fifteen of the eighteen pages— until page sixteen when he wrote, "From here in I am somewhat confused."

Still, Farley had read it and liked parts of it using words like:

"Great!"

"Good!"

"This is wonderful!"

"Fantastic!!!"

But he didn't rework it and didn't write anything else.

Then he up and moved to Colorado on a whim. He became a ski bum and in seven years wrote exactly one four-line poem about the sound his skis made scraping ice.

He didn't have the desire to write. Why?

He had kept reading though, so in a way it was like he was keeping oxygen and nourishment flowing to something alive, like a spore that he always thought would be released, would find the right conditions to grow.

Then his twenties were over and he was thirty and still basically a ski bum. He met a girl and together they started chasing the idea that they could run a restaurant. He knew it was a bust, but he kept up the chase until the bitter end, until the idea and the girl were gone and he got drunk and went skiing and lay wounded in *the deep powder of his vanished life and he thought, Maybe one day I will write about this, as the snowmobile dragged him away.*

It was only then that he began to write again, once it was all really over and he had moved back home to Chicago. The writing began almost by accident one day. Like an ace he had been carrying fell out of his sleeve. One night in October he found a website dedicated to Chicago Bears fans called Between The Columns. There was an open call for articles. After the Bears came from behind to beat the Cardinals on Monday night, he stayed up and wrote an article entitled, "Significant Ass Crownings in History." The article got published. His new girlfriend was surprised. "I didn't know you wrote," she said.

So he wrote some more. And the website kept publishing his work. And then they hired him and he wrote an article a week for the rest of the season, as the Bears rolled into the Super Bowl. Following a week 12 loss to the Patriots, his article, "Things Grosser Than Grossman's Interceptions," managed a small syndication. But then something swallowed the website, a buyout of some kind with a noncompete clause. It was shady. His preview for the Superbowl went unpublished and his email bounced back. He had nowhere to write.

That's when the first kid came along. He waited tables at a nice restaurant and made decent money. And so began his practice of looking back at his twenties wistfully.

*

It continued into the night. He would drift off, start to dream, and then his heart would wake him up. He tried sitting up when the palpitations got stronger and this seemed to help but they never went away. Lub-dub… DUB… DUBDUB… Lub-dub. And each time he glanced at the windows. The planet switched windows: first from the left to the middle, then from the middle to the right. Stars disappeared and new constellations appeared. Then the planet was gone. Which planet was it?

4. The isolation has fostered the development of 150 unique species of fauna and flora, endemic to the island. Endemic means only on the island.

The publishing business. It was an impenetrable fortress. Gates and walls. Moats with alligators. You had to be very good and very persistent and then very lucky. He knew that he had some talent and thought that if he really worked at it he could develop it into something real, and he knew he would be persistent. If he was alive he would write. He knew that now. If he kept living, he would keep writing. It was a system he had developed. The living fed the writing and vice versa. What was the term? He had studied it in biology. Ah, yes. Symbiosis. But that involved two organisms.

What worried him was that he would never be lucky. That he might work really hard, constantly, but just never get the break. It happened. Surely it did.

And the agents. He had seen their faces on the internet and read their articles and interviews. You couldn't blame them, really. It was a business. You didn't become successful in a cutthroat business by taking a lot of chances. You could take some chances but, like in anything involving gambling, you had to be very careful and sparing with chances. But you could not pin it all on the agents, as if they bore full responsibility. Like if they just all stood up together and said, No. No to bad books and the same formulas and the safe authors with safe books. And then pigs could start delivering books to independent bookstores via airmail. This was the kind of thinking he did when he could not sleep, and he knew it was unoriginal.

He had read once that you should think of an agent as a catcher in baseball that really wants to catch what you're pitching; you just have to pitch it the right way. He had tried to think of it that way. He had tried to think of it in a lot of ways, because he got tired of the other way of thinking.

And the letters. Queries, they were called. How many had he written? A hundred? More? Well, at least he had tried. And there were some decent letters. Maybe he could publish a book of all his query letters? He did work hard on them. His voice was there. The voice he had been looking for, trying to develop. It was in those query letters. There's your irony and pity right there.

How To Get Published. All those writer's self-help books. A lot of good they did. Sending off stories on Submittable, one or two a week. Keeping a log of submissions. Very organized. Opening the email account every day with just the faintest trace of hope. Today could be the day. Maybe. And then the same old emails. Checking throughout the day, often three or four times. Each time, opening the email brought just a tiny feeling of being crushed, stepped on, ignored, defeated. A little flick of despair. The form letters. He could spot them right away. Thank you very much for submitting. Unfortunately…

But that's the writer's life. You have to be tough. Persistent. Thick-skinned. And he was all those things. But now his thick skin was starting to be wrinkled, too.

The book architect that wanted eight hundred dollars. Story contests that cost twenty dollars. Reading fees three dollars. Writing classes. Clubs. A halffilled out low-residency MFA application. Whatever it takes. Whatever it takes? Whatever.

*

He was dreaming now and fishing with his grandfather and father in Canada. He was maybe twelve years old and drinking coffee for the first time with lots of milk and sugar because they were waking up so early.

They set out in the blue dawn darkness and the water was black. The guide was Native American and smoked constantly. The boat rushed out and the wind was very cold and fierce. The guide cupped his cigarette in his hand because of the wind. Then they stopped and the guide smoked and the fishing began. It was very quiet and still. He watched the smooth glassy surface of the water and the red rocks and vegetation of the shore. Far off, they heard a loon crying. They fished all morning for walleye and didn't get a bite. The sun came out and they took jackets off and went to another spot, the guide always smoking, shielding the wind with his hand when they were moving. But no bites. If they didn't catch a walleye soon they would have to eat cold cut sandwiches for lunch.

But then he got a bite. He pulled it in and it broke the line just as he pulled it over the edge of the boat. It was a large walleye and everyone would have enough fish for the shore lunch. His dad and grandfather were very happy, both to have fish for lunch but also that he was the one to have caught it. But it flopped around the boat horribly. It made a loud thudding sound and kept flopping about, frantically trying to get back to the water as its body's cells screamed for oxygen. But it couldn't get back. And the guide couldn't get a hold on it. The walleye kept flopping around and that's when he woke up and felt his heart, just like the fish in the boat from his dream.

*

And what is it really? The need to write. Like a need for attention? Recognition? Some kind of redemption for all those hours reading alone. Seriously, he asked himself, how many Tolstoy novels did you read during your twenties? What the hell was it for? You could read Tolstoy in your seventies! Why spend your precious youth hopelessly lost on page 296 of Anna Karenina? Time you can never get back.

Or all those nights sitting on the couch with the lamp over his shoulder, pretending the couch was like a ship, crossing a vast sea. It was a romantic idea. Idealistic. But now, it seemed to him, like hiding, avoiding.

And the dictionary held together by duct tape: words words words. But in the end, what did they all mean, after all? And now, when he would see the dictionary, it was like words had let him down, betrayed him.

In college a journalism professor Sal Stevens, in a class called Magazine Reporting, had been impressed by his work. Sal was a Big Shot Journalist. Tough, brash, East Coast. He had been published in all the big magazines. Had a book. Always had things cooking, as he would tell his students, name-dropping a celebrity he had just interviewed.

Sal Big Shot Stevens often had him read his papers to the class. It was embarrassing. The other students clearly resented it. But Sal kept sending him up to read each assignment. "Notice the active verbs," the professor would say. Or, "Pay attention to how each sentence is supported and not floating in space, like many of the ones I read this weekend." He was condescending like that, putting down students and in the next breath talking about his own writing achievements. One time before Sal Big Shot Stevens called him to read his assignment, Sal said, "This next one sounds a bit like Hemingway— if any of you have ever heard of him."

He met Sal Big Shot Stevens during his office hours. The professor said, "You should be writing for more than just my class. Why not get out there and get something published?"

With a shrug, an arrangement was made. He would write a story and Sal Big Shot Stevens would help him to get published.

So he wrote a story about a ski trip over a spring break. It was called, "On Top Of The World." And really, what could even a Big Shot Journalist do with something like that?

But something else changed. The professor put it together that his father was Richard Stevenson, the state superintendent of instruction in Illinois.

In that moment the professor seemed to be looking at him differently, seeing him in a new light, the light of privilege, revealing a spoiled Holden Caulfield brat on a ski trip.

And then there was the debacle of his final project, his portfolio. He had procrastinated and then turned it in at literally the last minute, disorganized, all out of order. The professor had given him a B+ for the semester. He thought about the twenty-odd students who had to sit there and listen to his papers, what they would have thought if they found out that he got a B+. That he wasn't the Talented Future Big Shot Journalist and instead in many ways was coming up A Day Late and A Dollar Short. That he was lost. And scared.

*

5. "We have not lost the connection to our island birthplace… the cord is still tied."
    —Julie Tumamaite-Stenslie, Island Chumash Descendent

*

He rolled over and she was awake.

"How is Maya?"

"She is asleep now," his wife said without rolling over.

"Has she been keeping you up?"

"No. She slept until three and I just fed her."

He lay awake and listened to his wife's breathing. He looked out the windows and there were stars again, different stars than before. A different window was blank this time, and the planet was long gone.

This is the whole world, he thought. The stars and my wife breathing and the baby sound asleep down the hall. Two other daughters sleeping peacefully in the next room. Why is that so hard to write? But it was. It was elusive. There was something that he could not capture, this sense of peace and belonging and home that the whole world sought.

He had it, and somehow it was not enough. He listened to his wife's breathing and felt a sudden, strong palpitation in his chest.

Perhaps it would be best if he gave writing up? Just focus on his job and being a dad. That was enough, surely. Maybe he would be happier. Happier. Why the *-er*? Just be happy. Count your blessings. One day at a time. Become a cliché that heals all wounds.

But he couldn't give it up. Like a child grasping a parent's hand, refusing to let go. It gripped him, he thought, just as he gripped it.

*

Then an A+ in a course called Literary Journalism his senior year. It was mostly literary and not much journalism. He still had that sort of chip on his shoulder. He remembered two of the stories he wrote, both profiles: one about a woman named Olga and then the other about his roommate, Gene Brinkmeyer.

Olga was an eighty-year-old Polish woman that lived in Bloomington. She was blind and had two tiny black eyes just like shiny buttons. And a puff of white hair, like cotton candy. He remembered that all these years later, that he had written that about her eyes and hair.

He visited her as part of an outreach program to the elderly. He would go once a week and read to her from his volume of The Complete Works of Oscar Wilde. *Looking back, it seemed silly that he would read Oscar Wilde and not ask her if she had any preference, or at least find out what she might be interested in, but Olga never complained or said a word edgewise. She just sat back behind those button eyes and listened. Maybe she dozed.*

But Olga also told him stories, what would become the crux of his essay. She talked about fleeing Poland by train as the Nazis invaded, the sound of bombs in the distance getting closer, and then finally a bomb landing on the tracks a mile ahead so that they had to get out and walk, carrying whatever they could. She had been pregnant at the time. Finally making it south to Hungary and all about her life there during the war as a single mom. Then emigrating with her sister to the United States, landing in Indianapolis with her daughter April, who still lived with her and brought us lemonade and snacks during Oscar Wilde stories like "The Sphinx Without a Secret."

And then the profile about Brinkmeyer, his roommate studying film who also worked at Victoria's Secret. When he would leave for work he would say, "I'm off to fold panties." He interviewed him while Alfred Hitchcock's Notorious *played in the background. So he spliced the interview with scenes from the movie and left out the part about the panties. The instructor liked it. So did Gene.*

"You're the only one I know that does anything creative," Gene had said. "We should do a movie together sometime."

His Literary Journalism instructor was a woman named Carol Grove. She had a successful career in magazines as a writer and editor, including Mother Jones, Esquire, *and the* Progressive. *She had a few books published as well, and didn't act like a Big Shot Journalist. Also, she was one of two people that asked him what his plans were for the future.*

"You should look into getting an MFA," she had said during office hours. And then in his letter of recommendation, which he wasn't supposed to open, she had written, "In a classroom full of soaring imaginations, his soared the highest." Which always made him think of Kid Icarus.

6. Millions of people live less than a hundred miles away, but here, you are alone with jagged beauty.

The oldest, their six-year-old, had a bad dream. His wife went into her bedroom and calmed her down. There had been a rattlesnake at school, and she had been having bad snake dreams this week. Their three-year-old, amazingly, didn't wake up from the screaming. His wife came back and lay down. She mumbled about the dream and how the three-year-old didn't wake up and then fell quickly back asleep. He was awake the whole time. Wide awake, wondering which window it would be. Lub-dub, lub-dub, lub DUBDUBDUB, lub...

It felt interminable. He lay there, and there were no more stars out the three windows. A layer of clouds had moved in, almost like closing off or shutting down the one thing he had to look at, follow, and study. So he was alone with his thoughts and the uncomfortable beating of his heart.

He knew a-fib and could recognize its irregularity. But this was different. There was an intensity to the irregular beats, a strong, erratic thudding in the center of his chest. It wouldn't go away. It had started that night while they were lying in bed reading. He felt a few quick beats in succession, a flutter. So he took his heart medicine early and tried to "bear down" and relax, meditate. But it was no use. Something was off.

He had had six episodes of a-fib before, but none for the last eight years. For a three-year period in his thirties he had one or two a year. The triggers were predictable: cold water, too much caffeine followed by vigorous exercise. But then he found a good cardiologist that put him on a rhythm medication.

He lay and thought of their honeymoon in New Zealand, when they purchased tickets for a canyon swing in Queensland thinking it was like zip-lining, but actually it was more like bungee jumping into a giant chasm. He and one other person chickened out, he on grounds that the adrenaline might knock him into a-fib. The other chicken, a girl, after watching her boyfriend do it, decided to go. He had stayed in the viewing room and became the Only Chicken on the van ride back. It was more embarrassing when his wife went a second time, upside down. Walking back to the van, the driver, talking about a ninety-year-old that had jumped yesterday, asked him why he didn't jump.

"Just not feeling it today," he had said, not wanting to go into it, thinking of the novel *Lord Jim*.

The driver nodded as if to affirm his status as a coward.

He felt cowardly and regretful all that afternoon, but it didn't last. He didn't really regret not jumping into the canyon. It had kept him out of a-fib on the other side of the world.

"Sometimes discretion is the better part of valor," his father had said.

And he had been careful. He stayed out of the ocean for a long time, until finally he relented to his surfer friend Tucker, who was adamant that he surf. So he bought an obscenely thick wetsuit and surfed the two warmest months of the year, if you could call it surfing. His main form of exercise was walking. Going out in the mornings or evenings like an old man. He never really pushed his heart rate. He drank half-caff coffee, only once a day. And he took his medicine and a baby aspirin religiously (though he refused the old man pillbox).

But there was no avoiding the vasectomy procedure. He had to have it. Another kid was not an option, so he went. He took a Xanax but it didn't really calm him down. He lay on the table and the doctor walked in briskly.

"How's it hanging?" the doctor said.

His heart was pounding.

And now he lay, on the edge of sleep but unable to land, like a plane that just keeps circling, not really thinking at all, his groin sore, his heart beating on. Lub dub… lub… DUB DUB DUB… lub… lubdublubdub…

*

The story he wrote the summer of his senior year. A desperate Hail Mary toss for a future. His friends all driving to Lake George for a road trip. Come, they said.

No, he had told them again and again, each time saying he needed to work to make money, but the real reason he didn't is the story he was working on.

The story itself was a Faulknerian tale of a boy climbing the shoulders growing out of his sister's shoulders at night. His sister was having nightmares while their mother lay dying with cancer. Like Faulkner he changed POV, madly, like an out-of-control hose, the words flowing in a blatant stream-of-consciousness imitation. The boy kept climbing up and meeting different birds.

He sent off the story in the fall, along with the letters of recommendation from his journalism professors Carol Grove and Big Shot Sal, to two absurdly prestigious MFA programs. The rejections came in the form of postcards in early November, a week apart. The Hail Marys landed softly, quietly, unspectacularly, with the expected result. Dean Worchester, a roommate with a peculiar need to retrieve the mail every day and the only person besides two anonymous university admissions employees to read "The Branches," placed the postcard on the corner of his desk, without a word.

"I liked it," Dean had said after reading the story. "The birds were good."

And no Plan B.

What will you do? His friend Hollywood's girlfriend had asked him (the other person to pose the question) on the front porch swing, later, in the spring, after he had graduated and was hanging around.

"I don't know," he said. And he didn't. He packed up his computer, his clothes, two furry moths named Doubt and Insecurity, and moved and moved back home to Chicago to live with his father.

7. We do not inherit the earth from our ancestors, we
    borrow it from our children.
    —Native American proverb

*

The left window started to lighten with the first rays of daylight. He had been on the edge of sleep and, without realizing it, had been staring vacantly at the left window turning from empty blackness to a grayness, and finally to pale diffuse light. His phone vibrated, and he sat up to turn the alarm off. He felt his heartbeat, very faint and soft, but regular.

He lay back down for a moment. He was stiff. In his lower back he could feel the stiffness as an ache. The room around him was dark and his wife was breathing deeply.

He rolled out of bed and onto the floor to stretch. Gravity. An inexorable force, he thought. Between the vertebrae, the disks, eventually over time, gravity wins. Compression. He stretched out his lower spine with cat cow yoga poses.

He rose and closed the door to prevent the noise of his shower from waking the kids. Then he started his shower with a full minute of cold water. For a moment his dream flickered in his mind. Something about his father? Then it was gone. He was awake now and the gears in his mind were turning, the software and hardware up and running. He was thinking about his day as he showered. He had read the sub plans the night before. The lesson he would teach five times, the video on the Channel Islands and the short reading. Then lunch with Tiffany, Helmer, and Ericka, when they would spend the whole time venting and gossiping about their principal, the other teachers, the students, the school, the district. It was like rolling around in the mud. It was dirty, but it felt good.

Then he would have duty, or campus supervision, standing on the side of a street with an orange vest, saying "Goodbye!" and "Have a nice weekend!" week after week, watching the cars, making sure no one was coming with a machine gun. And then traffic and E Street Radio's *The Wild and the Innocent* to try to get out of his funk. The day was predictable. It was like autopilot, and he was setting the course now, soaping and shampooing. Once the course was set, his day would proceed of its own accord, like his body was a vehicle—albeit one with a sore axle.

He leaned forward and let the hot water spray his back. A daily shower. He thought, how many millions of people out there don't have this luxury? Refresh, he thought. Emerson said that. Or was it Thoreau?

He went into teaching to get back his nights and weekends. It was like his father's advice finally penetrated his brain, after years of bombardment, one slipped past his defenses. He considered getting his credential, but thought maybe he should try being a substitute first. He bounced around Chicago Public Schools for six months before landing a gig as an English teacher for a woman on maternity leave. He sort of liked it and that summer went right up to the edge of enrolling in a credential program. He subbed for another six months and that winter the third kid came on the same day as a polar vortex. Next summer they moved to California.

When they arrived in sunny San Diego, he subbed for a few months and fell into a regular job as a site sub at an elementary school. It was just dumb luck. His sense of humor clicked with the two office assistants, the people that really control a school. It was steady. It didn't pay, but it gave them benefits and was enough, with his father's continued financial support and his wife's part-time marketing gig. That was almost two years ago. Time was a blur. He kept thinking he should go to night school, enroll over the summer, get the credential that his father endlessly suggested, but he never did.

As a substitute, erasing his name every day, he sometimes felt like his name, his life, stood for nothing. He stood for this: sit in your seat and do your work quietly. He stood for busy-work. He did not stand for math, science, art, physical education. Not on a permanent basis. He was Mr. S., cracking jokes, a clown, a fool.

This was the most salient when he subbed for a Language Arts lesson. His life did not represent words or stories, not on a consistent basis. Even when he found the energy to write his slush …

8. Animals found only on the islands: the island fox and the scrub jay; miles of ocean, strong winds and rough seas to protect them.

Fridays were his reward to himself. Starbucks. He didn't need to make his own breakfast or coffee, just his lunch, which was usually a frozen dinner or a PBJ. Sometimes his wife would get him a prepared salad, or he would make a turkey sandwich.

He struggled in the morning. The kids were usually up and in his business. They would put on his shoes or want to pick out his clothes or ask for breakfast and then fight over which cup and which *Frozen* gummy vitamin—they each wanted Elsa, but then the bottle ran out of Elsas...it was exhausting. And every minute later that he left the house was five minutes more of traffic.

But not this morning. Everyone was asleep. He sat on the living room couch. This was his most philosophical moment of the day, surpassing his time doing campus supervision at the end of the school day. He would sit, sometimes for a full five minutes if the kids were still asleep, and try to wake up. He would look out the window at the quiet suburban street and let his thoughts meander over the meaning of his life. What was it all about?

This morning he sat down and felt, along with the soreness of his groin, the full weight of his sleeplessness. The pain and fatigue mounted him, straddled and attached, so that he would carry it all through the day. He would beat it back with medicine or coffee or food, but it would come back heavier. He felt it deep in his bones and in his mind. There was also a strange sort of pride, that he could endure, and that was a sign that his life did indeed stand for something of value that would go in an obituary.

That's enough morbidity, he thought. He put on his socks and shoes and reluctantly got up, packed his lunch of frozen mac 'n' cheese (organic!), and slipped out the door without a sound.

His first winter in California, as flowers bloomed and he longed for the dormancy and cold of winter, he and his friend Anthony planned on writing a screenplay together. Anthony told him about this new technology called Skype and they set up a meeting. They joked around for a while that he hadn't actually moved to California and that he was actually in his old apartment and trying to lie about it. They joked around a long time about it. Like people Anthony knew were in Chicago, like Farley or Shawnie, walked by in the background. Or like thunder went off at the same time. Finally they got down to business and agreed to each try to generate ideas and talk again in a week. Then they joked again that they should just do a coffee shop on Southport instead of him pretending to live in Southern California and using Skype.

He came up with three ideas: Mitt's Mitt, which was a Big Lebowskian one-thing-follows-another sort of unwinding tale, about a fantasy sports columnist named Mitt that gives advice that is always horribly off. The columnist is facing a life crisis of sorts: His girlfriend cheated on him, his brother died in Afghanistan, his parents got divorced, and he's about to lose his job because his fantasy football advice is so terrible. He has his grandfather Mitt's old time baseball mitt, from like the '30s, with his grandfather's purple heart from World War II. The incendiary event that triggers the plot is Mitt having his apartment broken into, losing his CD collection, a jar full of coins, and the baseball mitt with the medal inside. His idea is that the movie could move from this incident into a plot involving a Dude-and-Walter-and-Donny like search, investigating all the suspects in his apartment complex to try to find the mitt and medal, which really represented his own courage, something that had been faltering of late.

The next idea he had was called Or Get Off the Pot. *This idea was a romantic comedy with the main character a stoner that couldn't quit pot or make up his mind about whether to marry his girlfriend. He had actually written the first scene one afternoon at a library in Vista, after studying and taking notes from a book called* The Screenwriter's Bible. *The opening scene featured the protagonist shopping for running shoes with his married best friend and talking about how he wasn't sure if she was* The One. *How did you know if she was the one? And the whole time he's trying on shoes that don't quite fit him, or they seem to fit but he isn't quite sure after he runs around the store in a Ben Stiller— esque clumsy way, knocking over displays or bumping into little kids. "I just don't want to walk around in these shoes if they don't fit exactly right…"*

His final idea was untitled but was like a modern Shakespearean story about a character finding a ring on a bus and then his girl- friend finding the ring in his pocket and mistakenly thinking it was intended for her. This idea was very rough and undeveloped, but he thought it had potential. Sometimes he thought maybe he could combine this idea with Or Get Off the Pot *but other times he figured they were separate, and the second untitled one could be more of a drama if he could develop the characters of the groom that lost the ring and the bride that it's intended for. And some- times all three ideas muddled together.*

At the second Skype session, Anthony didn't have any ideas. He had quit his job selling diamond saw blades and had to spend the week working on his résumé. He shared only the first idea and Anthony thought it might have some potential. They brainstormed a list of suspects that would live in the shitty apartment complex.

The modern artist with pieces that all resembled futuristic toilets. The cocaine addict that talked openly about becoming a professional golfer and lived above Mitt and always had spectacular, intense shouting matches with his girlfriend, every word clear as a bell through the paper-thin ceiling/floor.

They agreed to talk again in a week, and Anthony said he would spend some time on it. He wrote a second scene, but it came painfully, with the stoner buying pot from a teenage dealer and avoiding the text messages from his girlfriend. He finished the scene, but not with a feeling of accomplishment because he knew he would have to rewrite it.

The next session Anthony couldn't make. Ditto for the one after that. And then Anthony got a new job at a marketing company and they had to shelve the collaboration for the time being, the being being permanent.

He always started the day with the Lord's Prayer, driving down the hill of his neighborhood.

Our Father
who art in Heaven
hallowed be Thy Name.
Give us this day our daily bread
and forgive us our debts
as we forgive our debtors.
Lead us not to temptation
but deliver us from evil.
For thine is the power, the kingdom, and the glory forever.
Amen.

Sometimes he would try to say it in Spanish, butchering the language like the character in *Love, Actually* that butchers Portuguese towards the end of the film… *nuestro papá en el cielo, tu nombre, que sea muy famoso…* Or else he would sing it with a Bruce Springsteen impersonation. But he would always say it, before turning on the radio.

Depending on the time, he might listen to satellite radio: a quiet song or some stand-up comedy. But at seven o'clock he switched to NPR on KPBS-FM in San Diego to catch the day's local and national news.

This morning he listened as Donald Trump canceled a summit with North Korea. There was an environmental group initiating a lawsuit against the city of San Diego for polluting the Tijuana River. Border crossings were down. A bill would go before the State Assembly this week to help create sustainable housing.

Then it was the traffic report from Torrey Peck. On some mornings, when he was feeling chippy, he would pretend that the traffic report gave him deep satisfaction, on par with oral sex. *It's backed up on the 8, isn't it? So blocked up. Horribly congested. Oh, oh, oh. Slowing now on the 15. Slow down. Yes. Tell me. Go slow. An accident to the side on the 5. Clearing now. Traffic moving in the left lane. Yes. Yes. Move it slowly.*

He knew it was perverted, but he also made himself laugh thinking, What if it were true? What if someone really got that much pleasure from traffic reports?

But not this morning. He listened to the traffic, and then the national correspondents came on to discuss the canceled summit in North Korea.

9. Rock cathedrals like the painted cave on Santa Cruz island are some of the largest sea caves on earth.

After he lost the Bears article, he was reading a book of essays by David Sedaris. It was like reading about a tourism destination, but to other planets. That's where I'll go next, he thought in the same naive way one thinks about travel but doesn't calculate any of the real costs or distances or time involved.

He began by writing about his Big Failure: when he decided to become a professional skier. He knew narcissism would be the trap to avoid in the writing, but somehow he ran right into it. There is a market for this, he told himself. People that wanted to make a change, a difference, to fix something deep within that's broken—only to fall hard and end up right where you started. It's relatable, the uneasy feeling that it's all wrong and only a drastic, bold move can serve as remedy. He wrote in the style of the classic young adult series Choose Your Own Adventure. *He called it* Choose Your Own Failure *and tried to make sure self-deprecating humor was the engine driving the narrative. Maybe parts of it did move? Or maybe it was one long exercise in wound-licking, pleasureless masturbation. He finished the job though, tenacious in his stubbornness. As he worked on the query that he would eventually send to a grand total of two literary agents, Neil Patrick Harris came out with* Choose Your Own Autobiography. *It was like he had spent three months crafting a tiny little match, a light he wanted to hold up for others to shine into their own fears about career and self, and the moment he sparked the light, an eclipse occurred, the light of a celebrity emerged, ludicrously outshining his small light.*

His thunder duly stolen, one agent rejected CYOF the next day; the other totally ignored it.

And so his memoir became like one more coat in the closet for the moths of his insecurity to feed on. Throw it away! Why hold onto something so heavy and stifling? What for? When would anyone wear that?

He read recently a book about all the reasons your book won't get published that said, "If you feel catharsis while writing, it's probably a bad sign." Well, he was screwed.

He stood in line in Starbucks and considered checking his phone. No, he thought, look out on the Brave New World of faces and morning and Life.

The old men on the couches were there, like always, drinking coffee and reading the paper and talking in a way that could safely be classified as banter. There were the same four or five guys, and always a new face. Where did they come from? How did they know each other?

They were all clearly well-off and likely retired. But they were still young in a way old people look when they are still very active and maintain busy lives. They knew his face and he knew theirs. He was the skinny guy with the school shirt and jeans that came in on Fridays with a personal cup.

Then the other regular Friday morning group, a men's Christian prayer group, sat at the one table for four. They all held the same thin volume. Something with "grace" in the title. Three of the guys were young; one was old with glasses and gray hair. One of the young guys was muscular and had long, curly hair that he wore in a ponytail. One of them had a carefully groomed beard and dressed very conservatively, almost semiformal with sweaters and button downs. Then the young guy with glasses. He seemed to be their leader, like he was running the meeting.

They were having a deep, flowing discussion, being vulnerable with each other. He stood in line and strained to listen, but came up empty. They were always speaking very earnestly, the others listening thoughtfully. It made him feel lonely in a way, wondering what it would like to be in a group that discussed serious things so openly.

It was his turn to order. His first words of the day to another person. Judy with red hair, the normal barista, was absent.

"Excuse me?" her replacement said.

He repeated his order, followed by an apologetic, "Not quite awake yet."

Speak with confidence! Then he was reading the *New York Times* on the newsstand, more about North Korea. He glanced at the televisions in the café, all showing different morning news programs. Weather. Sports. North Korea. Then he stood and watched the men on the couches, the group at the table, all talking and listening; he watched the gestures of the speakers and the expressions of the listeners, the nodding, a contemplative squint, a question, the back and forth. He watched people come and go, grabbing their orders or standing in line, on their way to work and school. Then his drink arrived and the sandwich barista called out his name and he was out the door, on his way, into the light and onto the next scene of his automatic day. He regarded the breakfast café, the hill with the sun rising behind it, and a lone gull high above the parking lot. He watched the gull soaring high above it all, thinking how this was an example of an organism in the correct habitat, one where it could meet all its needs.

10. The isolated beaches contain one of the largest rookeries of seals and sea lions in the world.

He ended up checking off every essay topic on his David Sedaris list. Being allergic to milk. The delusional years when he toyed with the idea of becoming a professional skier. His car accidents. His year as a sports journalist. The knee surgery after his accident. Waiting tables, the kitchen calling him "chiquelin" which he learned online meant "big kid." His satire: A Portrait of the Artist as a Substitute Teacher. The moths were growing fatter and fatter.

A creature of habit. He drove the same roads. He ate the same Starbucks sandwich and drank the same iced coffee with two pumps of sweetener and listened to the same rock 'n' roll station. With the food and the coffee and the rock 'n' roll, it was the one moment of his day that he really felt free, alive, singing his heart out into the dashboard, a feeling that would fade away when he parked and turned off the ignition.

But now he was a rocker, the sun was rising on the California hills, the traffic was all around him, women putting on makeup in rearview mirrors, people texting and driving, the rigid faces of people on their way to work. The inching forward and brake lights and bovine expressions.

He was on his way to work too, but in his mind he was young again, with his close friends beside him, and the song he was listening to was not written by a famous musician, but by him. He wrote it. He was the songwriter and the singer, belting words of truth and giving hope to all these faces in the river of traffic driving to jobs that didn't quite fit, lives imperfect with sad lost dreams in rearview mirrors; he was turning the rigid loose, stillness to motion and dancing, with words and notes like tips of arrows, landing and resonating and not falling or floating off like some lost ignominious piece of space junk.

But it was just that: a dream. He wasn't a great singer or a great guitar player or even a musician in a cover band that played in a garage. He was who he was. A middle-aged substitute teacher with kids and a mortgage. And he knew that this was something to be proud of. His family. That his regrets and sorrow were sinful in a world with so much hunger and illness and war.

Getting out of the car, he felt the soreness and smiled to conceal a grimace as young students greeted him enthusiastically like a character in an amusement park. He already knew his assignment for the day. He was Mr. Santos. He was teaching science. He walked towards the entrance of the school, slowly.

11. Ancient dunes reveal the caliche forest, fossilized trees from long ago.

*

"OK, let's turn to the article. Who would like to begin reading? Susan, why don't you start us off."

"Something in our imagination beckons us to the islands… Protected by winds and waves… A place of solitude and adventure…Out on the edge of the continent, out on the edge of the imagination…"

None of his David Sedaris-inspired stories found a home. He could see the rejections without even opening the emails.

"Thank you for submitting, but unfortunately… We wish you luck."

Screw it, he thought. My life just isn't that interesting. I'm not that funny. Fiction or bust. So he decided to write stories. He read every short story he could get his hands on, and wrote stories imitating the ones he liked. Tall tales à la Twain. Adventure à la Anthony London. Strange and funny à la Miranda July. He wrote fantasy stories à la Isaac Asimov. A world with two suns, both about to disappear in an eclipse that would last three hundred years. Would the protagonist make it to his grandfather's home in time? Just before he's about to reach it, a war breaks out between all the exoskeletons and the endoskeletons. His favorite collection of short stories was J.D. Salinger's Nine Stories. *He thought about all the stories he had from playing baseball his entire childhood and years of recreational adult softball. Plus, his thirty-plus years of being an avid baseball fan. He had a lot of stories. Not really baseball stories, but human stories. Nine stories, nine innings. He wrote and wrote and wrote. Every Sunday night, he would send them off into the universe.*

The first thing he did at work was get his assignment for the day (if he didn't know it), go to the lounge, get coffee (Monday through Thursday), put in earbuds, listen to music, and check his email on his phone. It instantly helped his mood. Usually Bill Evans piano or Wes Montgomery guitar, just something in the background while he scanned the usual junk mail. It was a way to feel productive, like not only was he working and supporting his family and being a contributing member of society, but he was also developing his ear and his musical prowess, or something.

Sometimes on Friday's he would go to Stevie Ray Vaughan or Jimi Hendrix or some rock 'n' roll, but today it was like the traffic report—he just couldn't muster it. He dialed in some Coltrane and opened his email.

*

"Sammy, will you read the next paragraph?"

"Feral livestock on the Channel Islands off the coast of Southern California pose a threat to many of the endemic species. For example, on San Clemente the population of feral goats reached eleven thousand in 1972. Once the effect on indigenous species was realized, goats were hunted and killed. By 1980 the population reached four thousand. The courts blocked a plan to shoot the remaining goats so they were removed with nets and helicopters."

*

He went through his work email. Next, he opened his personal email and right away spotted it.

The subject line read, "RE: Query—NINE INNINGS".

It was Kevin Gries, a literary agent he had queried a month back, tossed out in the night like a grenade from a bunker. With his stomach in his chest he opened it and read:

Mr. Stevenson,

I enjoyed reading your story about Jesus showing up for a senior's softball game at twilight. I think there is a market for your writing, and I would like to discuss representing your work. Please contact me at your earliest convenience by cell phone.

He read the email three times. Then he read it again. He practically waltzed to the science room, forgetting about his wound, and closed the door. He selected the Phish song "Down with Disease", turned it up as high as it would go, and danced around.

The bell rang. Students were outside waiting. He let the music play and flung the door open. Suspicious faces greeted him.

"It's wonderful to see you! I hope you are ready to learn about an amazing place just beyond our horizon: the islands off the coast of Southern California!"

*

When the last class ended he walked out to the softball field so as to have better reception.

"Hello, Kevin Gries please."

"This is Kevin."

"Hi. I am calling regarding an email I received expressing interest in *Nine Innings*."

"Yes. Glad you called. Really enjoyed your story, 'Check In On the Dugout.' Really good. The voice and pacing. I read your query letter and thought we might be a good fit for each other. I've recently sold some baseball fiction and I think there's an untapped market there. All those hardcore baseball addicts and weekend warriors out there. They've got money to spend and a passion for the game. From what I can tell with your query, if you've got more stuff like this one, I think we could really have some success. We'll have to change the title of course. *Nine Innings* is already taken. Don't you use Google? I'm sure you can come up with something."

They talked a little more. It was surreal, like he was dreaming. A fifth-grade PE class walked out onto the blacktop to play dodgeball. It was like he was floating, somehow, up above it all.

"So if you can get to the Palomar Airport by four thirty," Kevin was saying, "We could have you in LA for dinner and we can go over a contract. I think this could be the start of something really special. Looking forward to it."

He hung up and just stood watching the students, and it was like it wasn't real. He heard the song "Down with Disease" in his head. *Now I'm on my way.*

*

He got back to his classroom and called his wife.

"Goes to show what a little faith can do," he said.

Then he went to Tiffany's room and ate lunch like nothing happened, like he didn't finally cash in on that lottery ticket he's been carrying around his whole life, like he wasn't on cloud nine. They talked like they always did: Ericka told them about a disastrous morning assembly.

"Running over everyone with her voice like a bulldozer," Ericka said. "It was painful."

Then he was back in his classroom, showing the video one last time. The minutes crept by; he didn't seem to mind. *Now I'm on my way.* He walked around, reading students' notes.

5. A vibrant world teeming with life

3. A lost world beckons

6. Cloaked in mist

9. Isolated, overflowing with life

4. Anacapa, craggy and volcanic, with its iconic arch rock, historic lighthouse, wildflowers that bring its rocky soil to life

3. Santa Cruz, the largest and most diverse of them all, rough mountainous island cut by a massive fault line, 60 plants and animals found nowhere else on earth

8. Santa Rosa, rolls from the mountains to the marshes, sheltering rare Torrey pines, sandstone canyons, and vestiges of a ranching past

*

When it was over he went out with his orange vest and said, "Good-bye! Have a nice weekend!" to all the departing students and their families, but really he felt like he was saying, "Bye! Have a nice life!"

Then he was in his car, driving north, singing along with Bruce Springsteen, and for once, he didn't mind the traffic. He had plenty of time to make it to Palomar Airport. It was finally happening.

At the airport he met Kevin's assistant, a young woman with spiky blond hair, talking on her cell phone. "Call me Jen," she said, and resumed her conversation.

"Oh, good, you found it," she was saying, "Where was it? How funny. The whole time. Only a stone's throw away."

In no time they were on a small private plane.

The plane ascended into the clear blue sky, heading west. He could see the ocean like a sheet of fire with the sun setting beyond it. The plane turned right and headed north, still climbing.

Jen pulled out her laptop. "Just a few quick emails I need to get out," she said, typing away.

So he looked out the window at the traffic crawling along the coast like a long column of ants. For a moment it was like Kafka's central joke: Now that he was here, in the plane and above it all, he almost wished he could be back in the traffic, in his old life, so that he could take it on again, be happier, not be such a grump or a complainer, coming home worn out or sitting around with Tiffany and Ericka being negative, thinking it was actually quite a beautiful and wonderful life, after all.

He watched the land fade away and stared out at the ocean, smooth as glass, for a long time. He could see the faintest motion of waves, like the ocean breathing.

After a short time, he could see the Channel Islands, dark swaths of land jutting out of the flaming glass sea. He watched them and remembered from the video how they helicoptered goats off the island in giant nets. He tried to imagine the sight of it, a helicopter passing his plane at eye level, with the goats hanging down at the same altitude, staring at him blankly, the helicopter removing something that didn't belong where it was, that was harming what was there, but that couldn't be killed and now had to travel, fantastic and awkward, back to the fenced place it belonged all along.

*

The whimpering turned to crying but still she didn't wake. In her dream she was playing high school soccer again and her team was losing. Her parents were in the stands, and she remembered noting that they were holding her children and that their faces had anxious, worried looks. The problem was that her team could not find the goal. They passed and dribbled like crazy and always maintained possession, but the goal was not where it should have been. And they couldn't find it. The field itself began to contort and take on lurid scenes: a hallway in her college dorm, Wolfram Street in Chicago where she used to have an apartment, the parking lot of the law office where she used to work as a clerk. Now they were passing the ball around traffic and pedestrians and all kinds of obstructions, but still they couldn't find the goal. Then they were back on a field but there was more than one ball. Two, three. A dozen. Which was the right one? Then the balls stopped following the normal laws of motion and gravity. They bounced and spun like something berserk and alive and then finally disappeared altogether. Time was running out, and the crowd was cheering frantically.

They were on a vast empty field with no lines and couldn't find the ball or the goal. Her high school coach was yelling at them, but it was inaudible. Somehow her sister showed up and was really mad at her, but she didn't have time to deal with it. She had to get the ball back first, then find the goal and score. She just had to. Everyone was depending on her.

Finally the cry grew louder. The three-year-old woke up and came into the room with a blanket and an armful of stuffed animals, crying about how much she had to carry. For some reason she always had to carry her blanket and all her stuffed animals into the room. She calmed the toddler down and looked at her phone to see that it was already seven thirty. It was then that she noticed her husband still in bed beside her when he should have already left for work.

A CANNONBALL STILL TO FLY

The credit card company let me go two weeks before Christmas. They said it was the pandemic. No surprise there. I was in over my head. I won't bore you with the details. Ma's boyfriend Dale got me the job. They gave me these spreadsheets of customer payment histories. Never been much of a numbers guy. So it didn't work out. I done told Ma it wouldn't.

Normally I blow off a little steam when I lose a job. It clears my head. But it being right before Christmas and Ma watching me like a hawk, I laid low. Then the day after Christmas I lit out before dawn, walked all the way to the bus station and headed down to Baton Rouge. I needed a holiday. I figure once I get back, then I'll do right, as Ma always says. I hear it so much it plays in my head. Preston, do right. On the bus ride I kept hearing it. Finally I said out loud, I will Ma, right when I get back. My cousin Benmont picked me up at the station and we went straight to New Orleans, pandemic be damned.

We had a good time in the Quarter, right up to New Year's Day. It wasn't crowded—for a change. I was set to head back, but Benmont said he was on his way to Mississippi to help a buddy and could use a hand. He said then he could take me the rest of the way to Knoxville.

"What kind of help?" I asked.

"The usual," he said.

I didn't know what the usual was, especially after drinking all week with his college buddies that were anything but. Still, I figured my funds were a little low and it beats the bus. We drove up to Jefferson on New Year's Day.

I been to Mississippi plenty. A friend of mine went to Ole Miss and I'd come down for football games. And my Uncle Gordy lives in Jackson. Gordy's a bachelor and lives a pretty fast life that Ma doesn't exactly see eye-to-eye with, but still, as a youngster I been to see him regular and gone fishing. Yet I'd never been to Yoknapatawa County, up in the north.

Benmont picked up three of his buddies we'd been boozing with: Ron, Stan, and Steve. They all looked like they could've played offensive line. I sat in the back of Benmont's little two-door Saturn sandwiched between Ron and Stan—I never could tell them apart. Steve was the Black one, but the other two might as well have been twins.

We drove through the night. When we pulled into Jefferson, I thought we were back in the 1950s by the looks of the town. Wasn't much to it. A town square with a big courthouse guarded by some old statue. I was bleary from both the road sodas and the lack of blood flow to my legs. Benmont and his buddies sure can put it back. We pulled through the town at dawn. Not a soul around.

We stopped for waffles on the edge of town before heading out to the country. We drove a good hour before arriving at what Benmont alternately referred to as the "rendezvous point" or the "staging area." I assumed we were moving some college buddies' couch or furniture of some kind and thought the language was a little strange. Like some big secret.

But when we got to the barn, I saw that it was. A big secret. Nobody would talk about it, whatever it was, directly. This was the spot, and they were all waiting for it to arrive. I opened my mouth to ask what "it" was, but, being an outsider, I didn't want to make a fuss.

They were a jittery bunch, the other three that would be "helping." I had to repeat their names over and over to make sure I remembered: Mike, Howie, and Scott.

Mike had a cloud of curly black hair underneath the raggediest hat I've ever seen. An old fedora that looked like a hobo had worn it for twenty years and finally tossed it away. But it wasn't so much his hair or his hat that worried me. It was his eyes. Wild, crazy eyes. All bloodshot with this look like he was about to do something and only he knew what.

Howie and Scott were like his right and left hand. Always at his side, giggling and looking at each other like everything was hilarious.

They were all milling around the horses. A pretty strange bunch. Southern, to be sure, but on another planet. For one, they all had long hair and earrings. Then, their clothes. They all wore odd outfits: jackets that didn't fit, scarves that might belong to their girlfriends, jeans with rips so that you could see their drawers. Just an odd bunch that kept laughing and making jokes about the farm animals. We were sipping moonshine, but I think they were on something. Benmont said, as if this explained it, they were musicians. I couldn't tell if they were called the Broken Hearts or if their band had just broken up. They were playing horseshoes and making quite a ruckus teasing each other. I was a little intimidated, to be honest, like maybe I was getting involved in something I didn't want to be part of. I stayed quiet.

We sat around all afternoon. Someone pulled out a deck of cards and we played high cotton. It was just us men, the horses, the flies, a bottle of moonshine that never seemed to have a bottom, and four ladies in the deck. On this particular deck, the one-eyed queen of hearts was winking. I kept seeing her all afternoon as the sun slanted through the barn slats; her winking eye and smiling face seemed to know the answer to the mystery.

Finally, just before sundown, we put the cards away and one of 'em, Mike I think it was, went out in his pickup to get some barbecue. He came back and we were just finishing off the last of the ribs when the one we'd been waiting for all day showed up. A skinny fella with long blond hair and big teeth that went by the name Big Tom. He wore a leather jacket with jingly chains. No idea where he came from. Didn't drive a truck or a motorcycle or nothing. Like he just stepped out of the cotton fields, or fell from the wide open sky. Big Tom. He wore dark sunglasses, had a goofy grin, and for a while I wasn't sure if he was speaking English. They all kept laughing like everything he said was the funniest joke in the world. I'd never been with a bunch that laughed so much. Like hyenas. I had no idea what Big Tom was talking about. Finally, Benmont introduced me.

"This is my cousin from Tennessee. Preston Grinder. Here to help."

"Hello," I said.

"Are you a dentist?" Big Tom asked.

"No. I'm unemployed."

Big Tom started slurping, like he couldn't control the spit in his mouth. "Last Grinder I knew was a dentist. A real sonuv-abitch. My teeth ain't been the same since."

"Well, you don't have to worry about me. I'm no dentist."

He pulled down his shades and stared at me. The whole barn got quiet. Even the animals didn't make a peep. "That's good," he said. "The last thing we need is some loose dentist with a drill."

Then everyone busted up laughing. I did too, but it was all nerves.

"Is it ready?" one of them asked, either Scott or Steve.

"I couldn't possibly answer that," Big Tom said. "Not on an empty stomach."

Then he got mad that all they left him was coleslaw and beans. He gave Mike a hard time, but they all just gave it right back to him. Just a buncha southern boys, like they'd known each other forever.

Big Tom ate his plate of slaw and beans and finished it off with a jar of moonshine. We all stood around smoking as the sun disappeared beyond the woods.

I decided to go and call Mama. She had only left fifty voicemails and a hundred texts. We ended up like always. "Do right, Preston."

I figured once he'd finished eating, Big Tom and the boys would get down to business. But when I came back, they were all sitting around the campfire passing around musical instruments. Big Tom was a singer and played guitar, mostly. They had a harp, a washboard, a gut base, and a couple of empty paint cans for drums. The songs were the saddest, most loathsome tunes I ever heard. All about men on death row, cheating wives, grave robbers, and bad-luck gamblers. One of 'em about pierced my heart. About a lonely old mother living in a trailer park with a no-good son.

I started to doze. When I woke up the fire was smoldering and I heard voices in the woods. They were all laughing again, and I think they were getting high. Benmont knows I don't go for the Mary Jane. The stuff never agreed with me.

Anyway, they came on back and went off in their trucks. There was a full moon. I started sweating though the night was cool, like I had a fever coming on. Maybe all the drinking had caught up to me.

It was just me and Benmont in his Saturn, following. So I asked him what it was all about. Benmont couldn't—or wouldn't—tell me. Only that it would be over in a couple of days.

"Ain't nothin' illegal, is it?"

"No. Least not that I can see," Benmont said. "Look. Big Tom has something he needs to move into town. And it ain't ready."

"What in tarnation is it?"

"Don't sweat it," he said. He assured me it wasn't gonna get me in no trouble. "Besides," he said, "you're just the look-out." We pulled into a little hamlet with a bunch of duplex apartments. A pretty southern belle opened a door and before I knew it I was tucked in on a couch. I lay listening to an owl off in the woods, hearing Big Tom's sad songs in my head.

*

In the morning the belle was gone. Maybe I dreamed her. They gave me some grits and a cup of coffee. Benmont drove me back into the town and dropped me off in an alley right off the square.

"Just send me a text when the coast is clear," he said. Then he gave me twenty bucks for when I got hungry.

"What do you mean, coast?" I asked.

He looked at me like I was the biggest idiot this side of the Mason-Dixon. "The square," he said, indicating with his thumb. "When the square is clear."

I looked over his shoulder and saw that a crowd was gathered around the statue in front of the courthouse carrying signs and waving a bunch of flags. They had the Stars and Stripes, but also the Stars and Bars, which I didn't find unusual. I mean we were in Mississippi, after all.

He gave me some hunting binoculars and drove off. I watched the group for a time. They had a bunch of MAGA hats, and their signs said "STOP THE STEAL" and "DON'T DESTROY HISTORY."

I found a shady bench, sat back, and watched folk coming and going. I kept hearing Mama's voice. "Do right, Preston." I kept thinking I should be back in Tennessee, that whatever was happening here with Big Tom I didn't want no part of. I already done spent enough time in the clink and didn't want to go back nohow.

Trucks were driving around the square with the Stars and Bars and Trump flags. A man got out a bullhorn, and the crowd started chanting things like, "HONOR OUR DEAD" and "PRESERVE OUR PAST" and of course "MAKE AMERICA GREAT AGAIN."

Around ten o'clock I got a text from Benmont.

How's it looking?

Real crowded.

OK keep me posted.

Then Mama started texting about some job. Saying I needed to be back by tomorrow for an interview. I opened it up; and she was seeing my blinking dots and I was seeing hers. But just like always, I didn't know what to say. So I wrote, "Oh, Mama," and put my phone away.

That was when I heard 'em coming. Voices. On the road from Jefferson. Everyone in the square got quiet and looked off toward the hills. They came around a corner and into view: a Black Lives Matter march.

It was a river of people of all kinds, chanting with signs and banners. The folks around the square got quiet for a minute, like they were assessing the situation, then they revved up *their* chants. I texted Benmont a picture with the words, **Might get ugly**.

And it did. The river of Black Lives Matter marchers surrounded the square, so that all the Stars and Bars and red hats were on the inside, like it was the Alamo and the group's mission was to defend that lone statue of a Confederate soldier, some thirty feet above them.

It was tense for a while. There were a couple squad cars to keep the peace. A few more arrived, but they seemed to be helping about as much as the news vans that pulled in right behind them. The two groups stood about ten feet apart on all sides of the square and yelled back and forth at each other. I never seen so many flags in all my life. It looked like it was about to explode, when up on the hill I saw the state militia marching in. Rows of riot police with their shields and helmets. They strode right in between the two groups, with one row facing the protestors and another group turned in facing the crowd defending their statue.

I sent Benmont another picture. It was a tense truce, but it took. Both sides relaxed a bit with the shouting and name-calling. Everyone stood their ground and nothing happened for a half hour.

I was starving, so I went off and found a greasy spoon just off the square. They had a big sign that said: "OPEN. ONLY GOD CAN SHUT ME DOWN." I figured I could eat ten meals and the "coast" wouldn't be clear.

The place was near empty. The only customer was a mom feeding her baby in a corner booth.

The hostess, a bored teenager, looked up from her phone and asked if I wanted a booth or a table.

"I'll just sit at the counter," I said and hopped on a stool. She gave me a *suit-yourself* shrug.

The cook came out. I ordered waffles, fried chicken, biscuits, gravy, and coffee. The smell of grease had my stomach growling. The hostess poured me a cup of coffee like she was doing me a favor.

Mama texted me again, so I silenced my phone. I closed my eyes and listened to the mom and baby in the corner. The baby was laughing, and the mom was making a little airplane game out of feeding him. The protest, or whatever you wanna call it, was growing again. I wondered about Big Tom and Crazy-Eyed Mike and the whole loony crew that Benmont had us mixed up with. What could they be plotting?

Then I heard it again. I could silence my phone but I couldn't quiet the voice in my head. "Do right, Preston."

The cook came out and delivered his work: steaming waffles piled high with fried chicken, another plate of hot biscuits, and a bowl of gravy.

"Enjoy," he said.

"Thanks. I will."

He slid syrup and a dish of butter my way and stood back, as if awaiting my approval. I doused the mountain of food with syrup and dug in. "Mighty fine," I said. He nodded but didn't go back in the kitchen. He had a bulging stomach and neck like they paid him in food. He had big eyes, a round head, and reminded me of a toad.

"So whaddaya think about all this?" he asked, topping off my coffee.

"It's crazy."

"That's one way to describe it."

He leaned back and crossed his big hairy arms. I shoveled in a mouthful. Then he said, "As someone that has worked in this town for twenty years, I ain't shy about sharing my opinion. That there statue is no monument of honor. It was put there in the 1920s by Jim Crow and the Daughters of the Confederacy."

I looked over my shoulder and could barely make out the top of the statue, the white marble soldier saluting with a rifle by his side.

"Now, sure," the cook said, "some chancellor down at Jefferson wants to add a plaque to smooth over the controversy, some crafty words that try to please everyone but please exactly no one but his own inflated ego." He blew air up at the dark hair sticking out from his chef hat. "I tell you what he *should* do." He leaned down at me with his dark frog eyes.

"Tear it down. Blow it up. Melt the pieces for some staircase."

He turned his face to see my reaction from a different angle. I kept eating. He smiled at me, so I asked for honey.

He slid a bottle shaped like a bear down the counter. "You got one group of folks think by destroying that statute you're destroying history." He pointed with his hand at an empty booth, like a group of like-minded individuals were all sitting there having coffee. "But them folks are dead wrong. You ain't destroying nothing but a symbol of racism and white supremacy."

He filled up my coffee cup, though I had only taken a sip since his last pour.

"Now, sure, maybe there's another group thinks you should keep the statue because it's a way to honor the men that suffered and died on the battlefield. These folks will probably tell you the Civil War wasn't even about slavery. Right. And I'm Marilyn Monroe, back from my trip to the moon."

He slid the cream and sugar bowl down.

"All right, fine. Ya got some Butternut statue at Vicksburg or Antietam or some battlefield, built in the late 1860s or early 1870s. Sure, let those statues stand and honor the slain. But don't give me this argument that these racist statues offer a public value, honor the dead, or preserve history. Every one of these arguments," he said with a wave at the empty booths, "is flawed and full of more holes than that biscuit on your plate. Like you should judge men on the values of their time and not ours. Hooey. Go ahead. Piss in the wind and expect your pants to stay dry. These soldiers fought to preserve white supremacy. You want to preserve history, how about buying some history books for the library two blocks away?"

I picked up a drumstick and twisted it in the air, like an answer might be on the back of the fried skin.

"Look at that little baby down there with his mama," the cook said. "In a couple of years that kid is gonna start talking. When that mother walks her boy through town, one of these days he's gonna ask her who that stone man is way up in the sky. And what is she gonna say? The truth? That he fought to keep colored folks from being free? Don't you think the parents of this town want a statue in their square they can be proud of? So they can look their children in the eye and tell them that this person lived and died for something noble? Something honest? With dignity? Not some lost cause?"

I had finished. The cook was sweating. The fat around his neck was shaking.

He leaned down close to my face. His breath was terrible. "Every last one, ya hear. Tear down e'ry last one of them Jim Crow statues." He backed up but kept his eyes on me, dark eyes that didn't blink. Then he shrugged and put his fat hand on his face. "Now, sure. It's not a one-size-fits-all solution." He pulled at his grease-smeared apron, like that's the size he was talking about. "You got some statue in some small town, put there in 1872. Well, let the town decide. But these here Jim Crow statues, tear 'em out like the weeds of racism they are."

Then we heard what sounded like a gun shot. There was a rattle of explosions. I turned and saw smoke and people running. The baby started to cry.

"Tear gas," the cook said. He walked over past the hostess looking down at her phone and locked the door. Protestors were running past, crying out with fear. Sirens blared and riot police shouted through loudspeakers. "Disperse the area in an orderly fashion." As if.

"Stay calm," the cook said. "We're safe. Had my windows reinforced the last time this happened."

*

After an hour, the smoke cleared and the square was calm. Everyone had fled, and it was just the cops and some stateys. I paid for my meal and went out. I walked back to where Benmont had dropped me off. I took a picture and sent it to him.

Crazy scene with tear gas. Think someone got shot. Saw an ambulance. Quiet now though.

Good work Pres. Keep your eye on the scene. Hang in there! Home tomorrow.

My bench was roped off. I didn't want to be busted for loitering, so I headed out of the town to where I could still see the square from the hills.

I found a tree and dozed again, dreaming I was back in my cubicle staring at a computer screen. I woke up around midnight and saw the moon shining down on an almost empty square. There was one squad car remaining and I watched it drive off. I sent a picture to Benmont.

All clear.

Benmont texted back: **Be there in 20**

I walked down in the darkness to the edge of the square and waited. Thirty minutes went by. Then an hour. I was starting to think about just walking, hitchhiking my way back to Tennessee when I heard two big vehicles rumbling down the road. They had their lights off, but as they pulled close I could make out what they were: a wrecking ball and a cherry picker with something under a sheet. Behind them was a pickup truck with the gang inside.

As they got closer, I could see Mike driving the wrecking ball and Big Tom in the cherry picker. Steve was driving the truck. Everyone flipped their lights on and accelerated into the square. I could see Mike's crazy hair swirling as he leaned his head out. Big Tom was wearing his sunglasses. I started running, and when they stopped, I did too. I saw Mike's wild eyes and insane smile. He worked the gears and lowered the wrecking ball like he was playing with a giant toy in a sandbox. He swung the wrecking ball right at the statue of the confederate soldier. It went sailing past his head, like the stone soldier had never left the battlefield. The ball swung up and out, toward the moon on the horizon. Just before it blocked out the moon, it came swinging back, right past the soldier's ear.

There was a cannonball still to fly. Mike swung the wrecking ball again, the one the soldier had been waiting for. It struck him square in the chest and pulverized him into dust with a mighty crack. The boys let out a cheer like Yankee soldiers. Mike worked the gears again and swung at the base, knocking away the plaque the cook had mentioned. I could see one of the guys running with some tools and what looked like a new plaque.

I stood, amazed, watching it all unfold, looking around, waiting for the police, the state militia, the protestors, some flag-waving pickup truck with shotguns… there was nothing but empty streets. I even glanced over towards the greasy café, half-expecting the cook to be peeking out his door. It was all quiet.

I turned back to see the whole crew climbing onto the cherry picker and Big Tom raising them up. They got up to the platform, and I saw they had a hand truck with them. They slid the thing covered with a sheet right onto the empty platform. Howie and Scott donned welder masks and welded it right to the stone, the bright sparks lighting up the center of the square. In a moment it was done. They pulled off the sheet and jumped back onto the cherry picker.

In the distance there was a siren. I ran for my life and dove into the pickup. I looked back to see a statue of a man with a cowboy hat, rimmed glasses, a bowtie and checkered tuxedo, and a square guitar.

We zoomed off, making a quick escape. I was too scared to look back to see if anyone was following. Once we were out on a country road I leaned over to Benmont.

"Who was that a statue of?" I asked him.

"Ellas McDaniel," he said.

"Who?" I asked.

"Bo Diddley."

My phone buzzed. I didn't even take it out. Instead, I looked at the Man in the Moon, like he would tell Mama for me.

I'll do right this time. Promise.

YOU CAN'T GO BACK AND SAY GOODBYE

I finished lunch and headed out the door. I made it down the street and was sitting at the light when my phone rang.

"Hey, did you leave already?" Christina asked. "I thought you weren't playing until three."

"I told you," I said. "We're going to hit balls and warm up."

I could hear Ryder wailing in the background.

"For three hours?"

"It's an hour to get down there."

"Still, that's two hours to warm up. Do you really need that much time?"

Ryder was really wailing. His tantrums had been off the charts lately. The light turned green. I accelerated into the turn.

"I told you," I said. "It's Torrey Pines South. This isn't just any round."

"Can you at least come back and say goodbye to Ryder? That's what set him off. He realized you left without saying goodbye."

I changed lanes and swerved around a garbage truck.

"Sorry, hon, I really can't."

"You can't come back and say goodbye just real quick?"

"I wish I could. I'm already running a little behind. I told Ted I would pick him up at twelve thirty."

"Fine."

Click.

I let out a deep breath. Something I'll have to deal with later, I told myself. But not now. I'm driving to play Torrey Pines South on a perfect summer day. Life doesn't get any better.

*

Ted had borrowed his buddy's city card for me to use, so we were each playing for the city rate. Forty-five dollars. Unbelievable. One of the top courses in the world and we were paying less than what I pay for my Saturday round at Twin Oaks.

Anyone that lives in the city of San Diego proper can get a card. Talk about a perk. Not only do you live in paradise with the best weather and the best beaches, but you can play a US Open course for under fifty bucks. Outrageous.

Ted didn't live in the city. He had some rental property and used those addresses to get his card. His buddy had an even flimsier method: He was a teacher in a city school and used his school's address on his driver's license. Ted said every time he votes or forgets to pay a toll, the mail goes through his office assistant. Ted sure knows some characters.

But that city card is worth its weight in gold. He's always telling me I should finagle my way into getting a card, but I don't know. They're basically about as stringent as your average ski bum working a chair lift, or so Ted says. But I just don't know.

I reached his office in Solana Beach at the agreed upon time, twelve thirty. Plenty of time to warm up. I was already on those fairways in my mind, hearing the waves crash. I texted him.

He responded: **Come on up. Good news and bad news.**

Ted made his living as a therapist. How anyone could be depressed in Solana Beach is beyond me, but he's always busy. He makes a killing, in fact.

I made my way up to his office on the third floor of his building. You could see the ocean, beyond the tips of the palm trees, from his patio.

"The good news better be that we're leaving to play Torrey Pines South," I said, walking in.

"We most definitely are," Ted said. He was wearing golf clothes.

"Phew," I said.

"Just need to take care of something right quick," he said.

He laid it out for me. One patient needed an emergency session. And one patient was late for his eleven thirty. I couldn't help but feel my shoulders slump. I'd been trying to get Ted to take me to Torrey since he picked up his city card, five years ago.

"So what, I sit around for two hours and we run up to the tee? I thought we were going to hit balls, chip, putt. The whole thing."

Ted waved me off. "We are. We absolutely are."

"How? Your sessions are an hour long."

He smiled. "Alex, have I ever let you down?"

"Well, there was that one time when you forgot to pick me up after my sinus surgery…"

"That was twenty years ago," Ted said. "And both Big D and Freshy were in town. How many nights do you get to party with *either* His Royal Shagginess *or* the Fresh Baker, let alone both? I was hungover. I said I'm sorry. Move on. Now listen, I told you. We are playing Torrey Pines. South. Today. And we're hitting balls and chipping and putting before the round. I've got it all worked out," he said, and told me his plan.

Both patients were meeting with him over Zoom. Despite the recent mask requirements being dropped, they both liked the convenience, Ted explained. The first one, the late patient, was already on, sitting in a waiting room. Ted had told him that his Wi-Fi was bad, that his camera wasn't working, and he wanted to step out of the meeting to try and fix these issues. He would go back in, tell him that the Wi-Fi was real spotty and he wasn't able to get his camera to work but they we could still proceed. At which point I, me, a fifteen-handicap golfer that sells insurance and has NO BUSINESS giving people therapy, would sit in.

"It'll be a piece of cake," Ted said. "This patient rambles on and on. He blabs for the entire session, every time, like clockwork. All you have to do is nod and say 'mmm-hmmm' every five minutes or so. He'll never notice. And if for some reason, the planets are aligned and he asks a question or stops his endless meandering, just type into the chat that, unfortunately, the audio isn't working either."

I looked at him like he was crazy, like he would get sued, lose his license, end up in jail.

"I'll be in the next room," Ted said, "dealing with the other patient. We'll be out of here by one forty-five— at the latest. Plenty of time to warm up, almost a full hour."

Can't you get sued? Lose your license? Go to jail? All those questions were on the tip of my tongue, but I looked past Ted's grin, out the window, where I saw a ribbon of blue ocean. My mind went out to the gently sloping fairways, the breeze wafting through the Torrey pines … I needed this. "OK. Fine. But it's your ass."

"Ass, schmass. This will be easy. Some people don't want to get better. They just want someone to listen to them ramble. All you have to do is make little 'uh-huh' noises." He walked over to his laptop, clicked open a window, and beckoned me over behind his desk. There were two framed pictures. The first one was him with his two kids. It was a recent shot at a Padres game. The picture didn't quite fit the frame and I inferred that after the divorce, he had swapped out the family photo for this one. The second one was a knockout blonde named Angie, the new girlfriend, but not the one he had cheated on Stephanie with. That was Amy, and she was, according to Ted, ancient history.

"Seth, you still there?" Ted said into his laptop.

"Yes, Dr. Whitaker. I'm still here. Is your Wi-Fi better?"

"The Wi-Fi is a little better," Ted said, winking at me, "but I'm afraid the camera is still on the fritz. We can proceed without it, though, if you'd like." Ted raised and lowered his eyebrows like a used car salesman offering a deal.

"OK, sure, we might as well," this dude Seth said.

"Perfect," Ted said. "You were talking about your experience at sixth-grade camp, I believe?"

"Yes, that's right."

Ted motioned for me to sit. He gave me the OK sign with one hand and a thumbs up with the other and slipped out the door. I sat down with a feeling like I was getting on a ride that I wasn't quite tall enough or old enough or *something* enough to be on. But I fastened my seatbelt anyway.

*

Boy, was Ted right. This Seth dude rambled on and on about going to camp as a sixth grader. I barely even had to say "uh-huh." He had a regular-guy face you would never notice on the street. He filled up the screen like a bad actor reading a script he had read a hundred times. There was a note of hopelessness in his voice, like he knew he wasn't going to get the part but would read it again, one more time, out of some sad compulsive habit.

He told me all about how, as a kid, he was still coping with his mom's death and started getting in trouble all the time at school. Then when he went away to sixth-grade camp, how this counselor, a real pretty girl that was probably a high school senior or maybe a college freshman, Sarah, was nice to him. Affectionate. Nothing inappropriate or sexual, only generosity and kindness. He went on and on. How he got in trouble at the camp and they made him sit out during capture the flag, but she sat with him and played checkers. And when a big storm washed out the kickball tournament, she checked on him and brought him to the office for hot chocolate because the thunder was freaking him out. How he had to poo so bad on a nature hike and finally couldn't hold it and ran back toward the cabins but didn't make it and shat himself in the woods. How she found him crying and took him back and helped him and didn't make a big deal out of it or tell anyone what had happened when he showed up late to the play rehearsal.

It was at that point that I drifted off for a little bit, thinking, You live in San Diego; how can you be depressed? Go to the beach. Learn to surf and play golf. Ride a bike. Get outside. Listen to Jimi Hendrix. But I didn't want to say anything. I listened back in and he was droning on about how he had stepped on Emily-Something-Or-Other's sunglasses and she was really mad, but how Sarah the counselor lent Emily *her* sunglasses for the rest of camp.

It was interminable and I might have fallen asleep, but Ted came in with a bottle of scotch. We took three shots, and on the third he handed me a hitter. I was high-flying then. The scotch burned on the way down, but it warmed my belly and mellowed out my whole body. Then the weed floated me up into the atmosphere where I could see the Pacific Coast Highway curling down along the coast to the green fairways of Torrey Pines.

Ted went back to his other patient. A moment later, though, he came back in and dropped a gummy bear on my desk. He popped one into his mouth and started dancing around the room, doing his Mick Jagger imitation. The arms, the hips, the lips, the whole thing. I had to bite my tongue to keep from laughing. Fortunately, Mick danced his way out of the room.

"And that's really where it started," Dude said.

I held the gummy in my hand, about to pop it into my mouth.

"Dr. Whitaker? Are you there?"

I cleared my throat. "Um-hmm," I said in my best Ted voice. I guess it was good enough. I chewed the gummy as the dude started up again.

"I mean, I always go back to that moment and think, That's where it really started."

Again. Silence. I swallowed the gummy hard, held my breath. Finally, Dude went on.

"I mean, she was so pretty, so kind, so caring, but I just couldn't handle it. I was too tender, too vulnerable, and her kindness pressed against that wound. So I recoiled. And that's when the pattern started."

I felt like I should say something, type something, but what?

After another long silence, Dude continued. "I couldn't say goodbye to her. I couldn't. When the time came to load all our stuff from the cabins onto the buses and then head over to the mess hall to say goodbye to our counselors, I stayed on the bus. I couldn't go down there. It was like my feet were glued to the floor.

"Everyone threw all their sleeping bags and suitcases and backpacks in and went down to the mess hall. I stayed on the back of the bus and crouched down, hoping the bus driver wouldn't notice. He did, though. 'Aren't you gonna say goodbye to dem nice counselors?' he asked. I didn't even answer. Finally the bus driver said, 'Suit ya-self,' and let me sit there. It was a broiling hot day, and I remember the bus felt like an oven. I crouched down and it was like I was floating in the stifling air. Like time had stopped or was all screwed up. I knew I should go. I knew it was the right thing to do, but then the time was up and everyone was back on the bus."

I looked at him, this Seth dude, middle-aged, a little over-weight, unshaven, in a wrinkled T-shirt with a collar he would chew from time to time. He looked like he was sitting in the same room he grew up in, like he had never made it past some critical stage in development and was this mannish boy stuck in an adolescent wasteland, and all he knew to do was complain about it. How did Ted listen to this day after day? No wonder he charged so much.

"The bus started to pull away," Dude said. "I had this terrible feeling, like relief that we were leaving but also like I had swal-lowed poison. A poison that would always live in my guts, that I could never shit out."

He was really chewing his shirt now. I could see it was damp.

"And that's when she came running out. Out of the mess hall. She ran over and flagged the bus down."

Dude sat and chewed his shirt. The silence returned. I threw out an "um-hmmm" in the most soothing tone I could muster. Ted burst in, playing air guitar on his seven iron. He did the Chuck Berry duck walk right into the Pete Townsend windmill, then up to his mouth for a Jimi Hendrix impression, before he spun around and went back out the door.

Dude went on. "'I need to see one of the campers,' she said. 'He needs to return to the main office. It will only take a moment.' She called out my name. I still hear it in my dreams. She's in the front of the bus and I'm all the way in the back. The sun is streaming in, slanting through the windows, and her voice moves through the golden light like silk, like something so unbelievably soft. It caresses me, still, the echo of it, in my dreams."

I managed to raise my hand to muffle a hot scotch burp. It was a close one.

"She called me off the bus. That walk, in front of everyone, to the front—that was one of the longest walks of my life. Everyone assumed I was in trouble again. They were all used to me being called to offices for private conversations with authority figures. My feet felt like blocks of concrete. I somehow dragged myself forward, past Emily in the sun, glaring at me, still mad about her sunglasses. I remember I couldn't look at Sarah. I couldn't look at her eyes. I made it though; we got off the bus, and she led me over behind one of the cabins, out of sight, like we were heading back to the office, but then we stopped. I remember we stopped in the shade of some pine trees and the wind blew cool air off the lake. She was so pretty. Everything about her. Her brown eyes. Long, straight, dark hair. A perfect smile. Perfect skin. We had only known each other for a week, but we had this connection, this friendship. We made each other laugh. We understood each other. 'Weren't you going to say goodbye?' she asked. And I couldn't look at her. I looked at the lake. The dust floating in the air. The pines swaying. Anywhere but her eyes. I remember I could hear the bus, the waves lapping on the shore, but it was very quiet, very still. 'Come here,' she said, and hugged me. I squirmed out of the hug and ran. I retreated."

Dude Seth pulled his hands away from his face and I could see his eyes were wet. I thought he was going to start sobbing, but he swallowed hard, cleared his throat, and said it again: "That's when it started. That's when I started to run away from pretty girls, to run away from love, to run away from the thing I need most in this world."

The door creaked open and Ted, now with his golf hat on, poked his head in. He pointed at his watch and mouthed the words, "Time's up." He didn't walk so much as waltz over behind the desk. "Okay," he said. "Seth, that was brave of you today. We're making progress, really breaking down some barriers and opening some locks. Same time next week? I'll be sure to have my camera fixed. Bye now."

MANFRED RUTHERFORD JUNIOR'S LAST DANCE

I like the early shifts. People going to work, early flights, that kind of thing. I'm through with the weekend nights, the alcohol-fueled fights and drama and vomit.

It was a Friday morning. I had been killing it all week, so I was thinking I'd make it a short day, only drive for a few hours when the ride came in. If I'd known it was to the airport, I never would've taken the fare—not with Omicron surging and those storms back east shutting everything down. Like everyone else, the airlines don't have anywhere near the people they need working, and those storms were wreaking havoc across the country. It was an old-fashioned mess.

But the ride said San Diego, so I thought it was downtown and would make for a nice ride. I think it was the housekeeper, or whoever that woman was, who ordered the ride. She'd probably never used the app in her life until then.

I crawled north on the 15. There were two accidents in the morning fog. People in San Diego don't know how to drive in anything that's not clear and sunny. I reached the 78, and the morning rush hour was like a brick wall and moving about as fast. The 78 is always brutal, but whatever. I'd been up this way more than a few times. I followed my app around and found the address in a retirement community called Lake San Marcos. One of those over-fifty-five places that doesn't want young people around stirring up trouble. Funny way to live, if you ask me. I imagined a sign that said, "Only Boring Old Farts Can Pass."

All the houses were the same: small one-story bungalows. I found the address and pulled into the driveway. That's when I saw the housekeeper, or maybe she was one of those part-time care people that also cleans. Anyway, what does it matter? She was carrying a vacuum and a bucket of cleaning supplies to a little white car on the driveway. I almost asked her if she could come to my apartment. What was the hourly rate for cleaning a hellhole? I was in a weird mood.

She waved at me and said something in Spanglish. "Just un momento" or something. She set down her cleaning supplies and ran inside. On her first step, she kicked over the bucket and all the supplies went scattering into the yard full of stones and little cacti. I don't know why, but it made me laugh. Like what's the rush? Go ahead, put your vacuum cleaner away. I don't know. I'm an asshole.

She was short, about five feet, but large with a head like a lion and a mane of short black hair. I thought she might be Mexican, but what do I know? She could be from Timbuktu. She wore a white T-shirt, blue jeans, and white tennis shoes— likely her uniform.

I sat and waited. It took a while, so I went over and picked up the cleaning supplies. I'm an asshole, but I try to at least be a *nice* asshole. Some of the time, anyway.

The screen door opened and she called out, "Thank you!" with her thick Spanish accent.

"No problem," I said.

"He's coming," she said back.

"Okey dokey," I said. I stood outside to admire the large green hill above the community, looming below the ceiling of fog. It was peaceful, all right. I could see why people moved here.

She opened the door again, with a flurry of words. First English: "Looking for something," then Spanish: "es una boda no se como se dice en inglés pero el señor va a viajar a una boda de su nieto."

"Boda? Huh? That's a wedding, isn't it?"

I knew a little Spanish. Only a little.

"Ah, sí," she said. "Él quiere bailar con su nieta."

"Sorry, didn't catch that. Nieta?"

"Gran-dau-tur," the housecleaner said. "The wedding of his gran-dau-tur."

"Where's the wedding? The ride only says downtown."

"Miami," she said. She pronounced it, "*Me*-ah-me."

"Florida? He's flying?"

"Sí."

That's when I realized the whole thing was hopeless. I was about to back out, to tell her it's not worth him even getting in the car, when he came out. After all the effort it took just to get outside, I didn't have the heart to tell him to go back in.

First off, he was exceptionally tall and thin, even all hunched over. If he stood up straight—which might break his brittle spine—he might have been close to seven feet, at least back in the day. He towered over his cleaning lady. He used a walker and had a helluva time getting past the screen door. There was only one step, but they had put in a ramp. He took that ramp slow, easy, careful. There was no giddyup left in that step. The cleaning lady stood right behind him, like he might lose the battle with gravity any minute and fall over like a tall tree. Timmmmmmberrrr!

He wore an old tuxedo. In other circumstances, it might have been like a joke—it was faded and too short and the shirt had these ruffles and the collar was too wide for his old skinny neck and the bow tie was, well, dangling—you get the point. Here's this old guy, getting all dressed up to fly to his granddaughter's wedding. I'm a heartless bastard, but even I could see what was going on. So I didn't say anything about the traffic, the canceled flights, the Omicron surge that had the airlines in a half nelson. Instead, I grabbed his suitcase from the doorway and threw it in the trunk.

He took his time getting to the car. If there had been a snail on that walkway, it would've been a close race. He had a small head. What hair he had left was slicked back. There was a Band-Aid over a sore near his left eye. The walker had tennis balls on the front feet, so it hardly made any sound. I leaned against the car in the breeze and watched the palm trees stir. It was a nice place to retire, all right. Maybe I could get here—in another hundred years at the rate I save money.

He was getting near the car. I indicated the passenger side so that he would have more leg room. The cleaning lady got the message and steered him around the front. I thought of making a joke, like, "I'm going to grab a coffee; let me know when you reach the other side of the driveway," but would anyone laugh? I'm a heartless bastard.

He finally made it. I moved the front seat all the way up and opened the rear door. The cleaning lady helped him into the back seat. He was so old and fragile I thought his body would snap. She was speaking to him in Spanish, little things that sounded like, "That's it, good, careful, easy does it"— that kinda stuff. She got him in and buckled his seatbelt like he was her child. His pant legs rose way up to his shins. I could see he was wearing those tight old people socks that help with circulation, but even those things were drooping down around his skinny bare old man legs.

"OK!" the cleaning lady said to me. She folded up the walker and dropped it into the trunk.

I could hear she was breathing hard from the effort. I closed the trunk. Even though the morning was still cool, I saw beads of sweat on her forehead and perspiration coming through her T-shirt. She smiled at me and said, "Un evento muy especial."

"Sure," I said. "Sounds like it."

We stood there and all of a sudden I felt a knot in the pit of my stomach. What was I going to do with this guy when we got to the airport and everything was shut down? Would I just drive him back? Would I have to help him back into his house? What if he got hurt … or even died? I looked at his small head in the backseat, his eyes blinking erratically behind his thick glasses. The edge of the Band-Aid near his eye had begun to shrivel. There was a big gap between his thin turkey neck and that absurd collar. I noticed he had a huge hearing aid making his floppy earlobes sag even more. Oh, gosh. This was a bad idea.

"Do you know his flight number?" I asked the cleaning lady. "A lot of flights have been canceled."

She squinted, trying to comprehend, wiping the sweat from her broad forehead with the back of her arm. "Ah! Un momen-tito!" she exclaimed and rushed inside.

I looked over at the old guy and saw he was drooling a little. She came back with an envelope. "Para usted," she said.

She stood across from me, smiling. I opened it up. There was a letter and six twenty-dollar bills.

Dear Uber Driver,

Thank you for taking my father to the airport. He is 98 years old and we are so happy that he is able to attend our daughter—his granddaughter's—wedding! His flight number is #3089, 9:30 at terminal one, United Airlines nonstop to Miami. Please help him inside the terminal, where a flight attendant will help him the rest of the way.

With appreciation,

Betsy Rutherford Jones

There was a cell phone number on the back to call in case of difficulties. I put the letter and the money back in the envelope. The cleaning lady was speaking to the old man through the crack in the window. "Tienes sus medicinas señor," she said, "en su pocket si necesitas." He nodded like he understood. She opened the door, wiped the little spider's web of drool dangling from his chin, and smoothed out the Band-Aid.

I looked at my watch. It was six fifteen. We had a snowball's chance in you-know-where.

"Well, what the hell," I said, and got in.

The cleaning lady waved and we drove off. At the first stop sign, I checked the traffic. It was a nightmare. The fastest route, taking back roads all the way down to the 56, still had us getting there at seven forty-five. I checked his flight status and saw that it was delayed. Maybe he would make it, after all. I presumed they would have a wheelchair waiting. Still, at the rate this dude moved, it would take him thirty minutes just to get to the curb. Oh well, I said. Oh well. It is what it is.

I rolled the window down halfway and started off.

"How's the air, sir?" I asked. "I can put on air conditioning if you like."

He didn't respond. I remembered the hearing aid, rolled up the window, and practically shouted. He grunted and gave a thumbs up—but it didn't seem like he understood my question. I left the air on, patted the envelope full of cash, and pulled out of Lake San Marcos onto a busy four-lane road.

*

We had been driving for about forty minutes, making decent time on the back roads my phone guided us along, when I smelled it. Piss. I looked back at a red light and sure enough, his pants were wet and there was a little puddle of pee. Even though we were getting near the highway, I cracked the windows and let in a little air.

The 56 wasn't too bad. We eased along, but once we reached the 163 south it was a parking lot. Another freaking accident. The fog had lifted but apparently not high enough. I sat there, smelling the old man's piss, thinking This is my life. This is my life. This is the life that I live. Take a deep whiff and smell your life, I said to myself.

That's when the old guy started, I guess you could say it was speaking. It was more like mumbles or grunts. He was getting more animated, until I thought I might have to pull over and calm this looney down, when his teeth fell out. I don't think I'll forget that sound, his dentures sliding out from his gums and smacking onto the seat. Then his mouth made this sucking sound that, combined with the pee smell, made me gag.

"What? What is it? What do you want, old-timer?"

"Oooooo-zik."

"What? I can't understand you."

"Moooo-zzzzz. Kah."

"Moose? You want a moose? No moose in San Diego." God, I could be such a heartless bastard.

He shook his head like I was the moron. The traffic crawled. The accident was still thirty minutes away. He snapped his fingers and started clapping. He pointed to his big floppy ears and made this little dance.

"Mooo. Zzzzzzziiiiii. Kuh," he said, after shaking his bony torso in his own little puddle of pee. The Band-Aid was hanging on by a thread.

"Oh, music," I said. "You want to listen to music. No problem. I got music. I got all the music in the world right here on my phone. What kind of music do you like? Rap? Hip-hop?" I'm really quite heartless.

I turned on some gangster rap and cranked it up. I looked back at his gleaming white dentures sitting in the back seat, like another little passenger. I kept waiting for them to say something, maybe crack a dirty joke. I never should have taken this ride.

*

Forty-five minutes later, we got through the accident. It was after eight when we cruised under the bridge at Balboa. I thought, get this nut to the airport and he'll be somebody else's problem. We hit another jam downtown but according to my phone I would still get him to terminal one fifteen minutes to nine. The gangster rap was giving me a headache, so I switched on some slow jazz. I looked in the rearview and thought he was enjoying it, until I realized that he wasn't bobbing his head to the music. He was asleep. And, by the smell of it, he was adding to his little puddle. His flight status hadn't changed. Still delayed. Well, it would be someone else's problem.

Until we got to Harbor Drive. It was crammed solid. We sat for twenty minutes and didn't move. The old man was snoring away, dreaming of God knows what. What the hell, I said to myself. What the hell. That's when a traffic cop started walking between the cars. He was stopping at the cars. And I thought this pandemic couldn't get any stranger.

He made his way to my window with his sunglasses and robot face. "Due to complications, the airport is closed. We're working to clear the traffic. Please be patient."

"Closed? How do you just—"

But he was already gone, off to the next row of trapped losers. I picked up my phone and called Betsy Rutherford Jones. Voicemail. I tried again, got the voicemail again, and left a message.

No one was going anywhere. I pulled out of my lane, drove along the shoulder, and made it to the cell phone lot. Screw sitting here, smelling piss and listening to this geezer snore. I sent a text message to the daughter that the SD airport had closed and her father wouldn't make the flight. That's when the old man woke up. He yawned, stretching his wrinkled face, and sat licking his toothless lips.

"Airport's closed, old man," I said. "No flights today."

He didn't hear me. He tried to lean forward but didn't have the strength to move the seat belt.

"No flights," I shouted. I had had enough. "Nothing. No planes in the sky. The pandemic. Storms out east. Global warming. The media. The election. Everything is fucked up. The whole world is spinning out of control. What do you want from me?"

"Daaannnssss," he said.

"What?"

I turned around and saw tears. Frickin' tears. The old man was crying behind those giant glasses. He pulled them off and wiped his face, knocking loose the Band-Aid and revealing a dark, wet, purple scab.

I was the one that should be crying, I thought, spending my Friday stuck in this parking lot with your puddle of piss. Then he said it again, clearly and with a command of his voice I didn't think he had. I almost thought it was someone else.

"Dance with me," he said.

It was a low, grumbling voice. It scared the hell out of me. It reminded me of my old man, when he was real sick, a time I try not to think about. Then he said it again.

"Dance with me."

I covered my face with my hands and screamed with all I had. I felt better, so I did it again, and again, and one more time. I looked out the windshield at the seagulls on the streetlights. From deep down, it came up. Laughter. I started laughing, and pretty soon I was laughing my head off. I was crying. I hadn't laughed this hard in years.

"Let's get it, old man," I said. "Let's cut a rug."

I clicked on a station of top radio hits. On came this song called "Overpass Graffiti" by some singer named Ed Sheeran. Never heard of him, but the nearby overpass sure had some graffiti. The song had a driving beat, and I thought I heard the words "feel my bones."

"This'll do fine," I said. I cranked the knob and stepped out.

I swung open his door, the teeth still sitting next to him. "Let's dance," I said.

I helped him out, shaking my hips to the music. He stood up straight, stiffly, his body cracking and stretching that old polyester suit. He put his arms on my shoulders and I held his old bony hips. I was crazy, but not crazy enough to press myself against his pee stain.

And then we were grooving and shaking. I looked out at the row of cars stranded along Harbor Drive. People were all watching us, some holding out their cell phones, taking pictures and videos. "Get a room!" someone in a truck shouted. People were laughing and pointing.

Screw 'em, I thought, and gazed out beyond. The marine layer had burned off. I could see the harbor, all the boats, the skyline of San Diego. I held his thin frame carefully, swaying him back and forth. His old veiny hands on my shoulders felt like nothing at all. Like his body was made of straw, like if the breeze picked up it might blow him away.

I looked up and his eyes were closed. That's when I realized. I wasn't an Uber driver. This wasn't a cell phone lot at an airport in a world gone mad. I was his granddaughter. This was her wedding. The song changed but it didn't matter. The old man couldn't hear worth a damn anyway. He was hearing an old sweet song, and he was dancing with his granddaughter. His fingers gripped my shoulders and gave me a weak squeeze.

I'm a heartless bastard, but even I couldn't keep a dry eye.

THE TIME I MET
WEAVER MCCRACKEN

I didn't so much get out of bed—I leaped. It was finally here: the first day of the 2019 San Diego Writers' Conference. I sang in the shower. I used a new razor for an extra-close shave. I put on my best suit and picked out my lucky yellow tie. It was my big day, the day I had been waiting for.

Here's why I was so excited: Weaver McCracken, the legendary golf fiction writer, would be a keynote speaker. That was on day three. Today, day one, I had a pitch session with Weaver's long time agent, Ray Giese.

Everything was ready downstairs. The coffee, my bag, and my gleaming manuscript: *The Pull Hook Wish*. I poured a cup of coffee and rehearsed how I would greet Mr. McCracken. Honored. Humbled. Privileged. How I would express what his writing has meant to me: everything. I poured a second cup, grabbed a banana, and hit the road.

I had laid the groundwork. I had paid for the Agent Feedback feature, sending Mr. Giese a daring dream scene from my story, where my protagonist hooks shot after shot into the ocean, off the 18th tee at Pebble Beach, during the US Open, on a tee box that's turned to quicksand. A vivid scene sure to stand out from the slush. At a red light, I practiced expressions I could use in response to Mr. Giese's praise.

Also, I had begun a correspondence with Weaver McCracken himself. Months ago, when I first saw that he was coming to San Diego, I sent a hand-written letter, care of his literary agency, saying how much his first novel, *Home On The Range*, meant to me. How I really identified with his main character, the deranged and homeless Paul Dufner, who moves into a driving range cart shack only to start working and eventually start playing golf, playing his way into the US Open, achieving glory against all odds. It really hit home for me.

The sun was just coming up. I pulled off at a gas station and stood at the pump, feeling the day's first rays on my face, thinking about what it would be like to meet Weaver McCracken in person. The possibility, nay, the likelihood that he would take me under his wing, mentor me.

My tank full, I cranked the radio and gunned it down the highway. I guzzled coffee and thought about Weaver's letter back to me. His astute observation that I was a young writer, starting out much like he did, much like Paul Dufner, facing daunting odds. His letter, also written by hand, now posted on my writing wall, next to all the rejection letters, *à la* Stephen King, nailed to the wall.

I was going over ninety miles an hour, so I eased off the gas and turned on the cruise control. You have to take chances in life, but you have to be smart about them. Like Weaver McCracken, leaving his job as a golf journalist to write golf fiction. Like Paul Dufner, leaving his job as a driving range manager to qualify for the US Open. This was my chance.

I was getting used to risk. It was a risk sending Weaver my manuscript three months ago. And he replied! I remembered the feeling of seeing his letter. The Florida return address. His small, neat handwriting.

True, the feedback had been harsh. The honesty of a pro. His sentence, "I have no idea what this story is about," was a blow, like a knockout uppercut. But he took the time to offer specific feedback. "Page after page about a golfer's indecision over tucking in a shirt? You lost me after the third line. Maybe a hundred years ago people would keep reading, but today's audience won't stick around that long. Readers need a reason to keep reading, beyond a tucked-in shirt."

It had taken me a few days to recover, get back to writing. I dusted myself off, picked up the letter, flipped it over, and found his closing, in all cap's: "THE WORLD (OF GOLF) NEEDS WRITERS. KEEP WRITING." I rolled up my sleeves and got to work. I dove headfirst into the daunting task of revision. And now the manuscript lay next to me, in the passenger seat, basking in a square of morning sunlight. I took the bend in the road, gulped more coffee, and rehearsed once more how I would introduce myself. Perhaps at the Meet and Greet. Or maybe a chance meeting in the lobby?

Hello, Mr. McCracken, it's an honor to meet you, finally, in person. My name is Sam Smith, the author of The Pull Hook Wish.

Then a pause. Let the realization sink in. Allow the surprise to settle, before leaning in …

The road straightened out. Speed limits be damned. My future was down that road, waiting in a hotel conference room. Ray Giese was down that road. Weaver McCracken was down that road. At last, my future was straight ahead of me. I floored it.

*

I took the Hotel Circle exit and sped toward my destination. I was giddy with excitement. Plus, I had to pee like nobody's business. But it was the wrong hotel. I took a quick leak and dove back into my car. Another hotel, the same chain, eight-tenths of a mile away. I peeled out of the parking lot.

Even though it was less than a mile, it was all one-way streets. I got turned around. My navigation told me to get back on the highway, but forget that. I had a heck of a time finding the place. I wanted time to review my manuscript, to reread my quicksand dream scene before meeting Ray Giese, but now I would be cutting it close. Finally, I took an illegal U-turn and found the hotel entrance, the right hotel this time.

This was it. I was so excited, I had to pee again. I weaved my way to a parking garage, grabbed a ticket, and sped up the ramp in search of an open spot. I had to go up three levels before I found one. I almost drove past it, catching the open space at the last moment behind an SUV. I yanked the steering wheel to curl in, but cut it a little tight and swiped the SUV.

I jumped out of the car, grabbed my manuscript and bag, and hoped it was nothing. There was a scrape. I looked around. Nobody. I tried to buff it out with my sleeve. I spit on it and wiped it with some elbow grease. But it was there, all right. A big scar.

I looked at my watch. I was meeting with Ray Giese in five minutes. There was no time. I had to go. I had to take this opportunity, a once-in-a-lifetime chance. But first, the john. I really had to pee.

*

I made it just in time. They were still setting up the conference room, so I had time to relieve myself, check in, and catch my breath. One of the conference organizers poked her head out and made an announcement to the herd of writers huddled in front of the double doors.

"We apologize for the delay. The doors will open in five minutes. Your full session time will still be honored."

I figured I had time to open my manuscript, to read over the end of the quicksand dream, where Chip Grace is up to his neck, about to go under, when his caddie Silver hands him a sand wedge and pulls him from his nightmare. Just as Ray Giese was about to extend me a lifeline, a way out of my boring and miserable and lonely life. No more waiting tables. No more being the butt of all the jokes at family gatherings. No more Sam Smith the Loser. Look out, world.

A spot on a bench opened up. I pulled out my manuscript and sat down. I guess I was still a little out of breath, a little sweaty, because the writer sitting next to me turned and said, "First time pitching to agents?"

He was a young guy, in a black T-shirt and jeans, with slick hair and a slicker grin.

"Yes," I said. "It happens to be my first time."

"It shows," he said. "What do you write?"

Well. I wasn't about to tell him the truth: golf sci-fi. I don't want another person thumbing his nose at my niche market, a niche about to explode into the mainstream. I didn't need to hear another person tell me that publishers won't go near sports fiction with a ten-foot hockey stick converted into a fishing pole. So I lied.

"I write about the environment," I said. "Smack dab in the intersection between the economy and the law."

He nodded, like he knew I was full of it, another fiction writer with a pipe dream. "What do you write?" I asked. He had a short-guy complex; I could tell even though he was sitting down.

"Investment strategies," he said, not looking at me. But then he turned to me and winked. "Everyone wants to get rich, ya know?"

His wink creeped me out. I was about to get up, but he beat me to it. "Well, break a leg," he said and stalked off. I watched him move through the crowd like a vampire looking for a neck to suck on.

"It sounds very interesting," a woman said to me, sitting down and taking his place. "What you write. It's so important."

She was young with long brown hair and a pretty face, until she flashed a smile at me—she had teeth like a horse. She looked out of place, like a girl from the country, in overalls she had sewn herself.

"It certainly is," I said, looking out through the window at the clouds.

"It's my first conference, too," she said. "It's so exciting! Being here with all these writers. Everyone pursuing their dream."

"It certainly is," I said, and then realized that I sounded like a parrot. She laughed her toothy laugh, and I blushed.

"I'm nervous too," she said. "I've never been so nervous."

I thought she was almost too young to be at a writers' conference.

"Oh, I'm not nervous," I said. "I'm just … you know … anxious for them to open the doors. Why are they late? You would think they would be on time, with the schedule they have to keep today."

"Who knows?" she said. "I'm Amy."

"Sam. Nice to meet you."

"*Hug Yourself and It Will Be OK*," Amy said. "That's the title of my book. I write self-help."

"Oh, that's … good advice," I said, and gave myself a little hug.

She gave herself a hug too, and we laughed. I was about to ask how old she was, thinking about how I wished I would've come to a conference like this at her age, if only I had had the confidence. If only someone had pushed me, given me some direction, believed in me.

The doors opened. It was time.

*

Ray Giese was a large man with a head like a bull. He sat like an animal, too big for the little table they put him at, one of a hundred little tables set up in the large ballroom. Everything about him was thick: his bushy gray hair, his mustache, his neck—even his glasses. He was dressed in business casual: gray slacks and a black button-down. A real pro, calm and sure, waiting.

"Good morning, Mr. Giese," I said, offering a handshake before sitting down. "It's a pleasure meeting you in person."

He half-rose with a quick, hard grip. A squeeze of assurance. Kind, but with authority. His thick, short fingers were strong but efficient, his elegant watch a symbol of success.

"Good morning, Sam …" he said, looking down at a piece of paper.

"Smith," I said. "The author of *The Pull Hook Wish*."

"Yes," he said. "I read your pages."

Here it came. Time slowed down. Our eyes locked. All the other agents, the whole ballroom faded away. He opened his mouth, his lips, a little chapped. "I …"

I leaned forward.

"How can I put this?" he said.

Sentences danced in my mind. I … have never been so impressed … so taken … loved every word … Would he offer representation, here, now?

I jumped in. "Let me stop you," I said. "I just want to say I'm a huge Weaver McCracken fan. His writing has been so instrumental in my own development. In my life. I'm sure you recognize in my scene the influence of McCracken's classic, *Zombie Golf in Galaxy MACS 2129-1*, when they stumble into a dark-matter trap on hole 12 and a half."

"Yes," he said. "I detected something of the sort."

"And, I want to say, before we go any further, that I've read McCracken's autobiography, *From the Lip of the Cup*, and I know how instrumental you've been in his career. I want to say thank you, on behalf of all his fans."

He nodded. "I appreciate that," he said.

We smiled at each other. He took a sip of water and reached into his briefcase. Was it a contract? No. It was my pages. They looked worn from rereading.

"Your story," he said, and leaned back. "I …" He crossed his arms.

I was on the edge of my seat. The edge of the edge. Here it came.

"I found it hard to follow," he said.

I felt myself frown, sinking back, the chair catching me in a way.

"All these pages about quicksand," he said. "The character going down and down. I have to confess, I started skimming pretty quick. There doesn't seem to be a bottom. Is this the beginning of your story?"

My mind reeled. Two hundred and fifty dollars for skimming? I wanted to turn and run. This was the advanced session? We paid extra for feedback. I glanced around at all the other writers having professional conversations. The agents smiling. The writers nodding. A back and forth. *Skimming?* It felt like an imposter Ray Giese. Wasn't this the man that recognized the potential of golf sci-fi? How did he not see it, here, now? Right under his thick nose.

"Well, no," I said. "It's not the *beginning* beginning. Like … of the story."

He licked his thick, chapped lips.

"It's the beginning of Chip Grace's descent into madness. His fall from grace, so to speak. Sort of like the golf sci-fi version of *Hamlet*."

His eyes blinked behind his lenses. They seemed to get farther away, like they were receding into his face.

I went on. "All his wishes have come true …" I started to have the feeling that my own chair was sinking down into the carpet, that I was looking up at Ray Giese, the face I had seen on my computer screen, receding to a great height. "But he's struggling … he's struggling to find … to express … to … identify …"

"There's some captivating images in here," Ray Giese said, his voice faraway, like from the top of a mountain. "Some really nice language. I can see you have a flare for the sentence."

"A flare for the sentence," I said, the carpet now up to my waist.

"Allow me to give you some advice," he said. I wasn't speaking to a man, to an agent I had stared at on my computer screen, that I had a written a draft of an email to, accepting his offer of representation. I was speaking to a great, dark thunder cloud, billowing up in the sky.

"When you give an agent something to read in a session like this," the thunder said, "you want to give the beginning of your story."

I nodded, feeling the carpet rising up to my chest.

"You don't want to pick a scene at random, even if you feel it's your strongest scene," the thunder went on, spiraling and swirling, coming down on me. "Agents read with an eye for the market. We've trained ourselves to find stories that will hook readers."

I loosened my lucky yellow tie, the carpet up to my neck. The cloud rushed down at me, burst.

"Where does your story start?"

My voice sounded tinny. I felt my mouth open, but I'm not sure words escaped my throat. Ray Giese handed me my pages.

"Find the beginning of your story," he said. "Start there."

I nodded, heard myself say thank you. I slid off the chair, to avoid being swallowed by the carpet. I moved, as if on an automatic sidewalk, past tables of writers and agents, deep in writerly conversations. I reached the door. I looked down at my watch. I still had five minutes left of paid time with Ray Giese. I hovered in the doorway. Half of me wanted to rush back, to clear up the misunderstanding. Maybe if I read the beginning, maybe he would see how it all fit together, the quicksand, the madness. The other half of me wanted to run. Get out of there. Disappear. I closed my eyes. I listened for a voice to tell me what to do, where to turn. And a voice came.

It was my bladder. It said, "Go pee."

I staggered out, past all the eager, expectant writers waiting for the next session. I made it to the bathroom but couldn't squeeze out a drop.

*

I found a bench and collapsed, dazed, shaken. I watched all the writers and agents and editors and publishers. It was a strange aquarium. I didn't belong here. What a fool I had been. A writer. Sheesh. That's when I remembered the scratch. I had scraped a car on my way in. The owner might be in this hallway. I should write a note, go put it on the windshield. But I couldn't get myself to budge.

The pitch session I had been attending ended. All the writers walked out, moving briskly, heading to the next seminar. In the herd, someone stopped, looked over. It was Amy. She smiled her horse-tooth smile at me and flashed a thumbs up and down to ask how it went. I gave her the thumbs down. She shrugged and made a little hug yourself gesture.

I obliged her and, oddly, felt better. I started thinking. Ray Giese was right. I didn't know not to send a scene from the middle of my story, but it made sense. He had no foothold, no way of grabbing onto a story hurtling along at such a pace. Of course it was hard to follow! Him saying that, I realized, was not an insult at all. It was a compliment! Sure, if it was some slow plodding tale and I had dropped him in the middle, it would be easy to follow. But not *The Pull Hook Wish*.

My mind started leaping steps ahead. I would need to rewrite my acceptance email to Ray Giese, to explain, show under-standing. No hard feelings. No damage had been done to our professional relationship. That's when I realized. I had signed up for a session that was in progress: Query Writing 101. Not only had I signed up, I had paid extra to have my query letter evaluated.

I pulled out my orientation folder, analyzed the map, figured out where the session was. I grabbed my bag and my manuscript and tightened my lucky yellow tie. I hustled down the hallway, remembering I still had my ace in the hole. I still had a chance to meet Weaver McCracken.

*

I eased into the query session, already in progress. Elizabeth Bloom, a top agent from a top agency, was up at the podium, listening as a volunteer from the audience read my query. I made my way to the back, found a seat, closed my eyes. It was the third paragraph, one I knew by heart, the part where I drive it home. It sounded new, hearing a stranger read it.

> Ten years later, Chip and Florence Grace are off to New Zealand to celebrate their anniversary. A love that began by chance, with Chip's pull hook that shattered Flo's bedroom window, once again falls into Fate's crosshairs. Chip is off golfing one morning and pulls a hook into the woods. He happens upon a wanderer, a vagabond who pulls three balls from the mud and offers Chip three wishes. Chip wishes to be young again, to go back in time, and to never pull a hook again. His three wishes are granted, but he realizes that if he can't pull a hook, he won't meet Flo in the same circumstances.

Will Chip choose his perfect life, always in the fairway, or will he come up with a way to hook one out of bounds to meet the love of his life? Golfers know that life is full of choices. Which club to hit? To play a flop or a run? Go for the green in two or lay up? In the PULL HOOK WISH, Chip Grace faces the ultimate choice: SUCCESS or LOVE.

It's been a hundred years since P.G. Wodehouse dazzled audiences with his golf tales. Now, on the heels of the great Weaver McCracken, comes a new voice ready to carry the torch in the great tradition of golf storytellers.

Thank you for your consideration.

I opened my eyes. A hush fell over the room. They were obviously impressed. A few were scrawling notes, likely taking note of the voice, the flow; the clear, hardened query of a professional.

"Anyone have any feedback for the writer?" Elizabeth Bloom asked.

Silence reigned. What could they add? A few bodies squirmed, clearly in an effort to come up with a quibble, some minor flaw in punctuation or tense that they could hone in on to impress Elizabeth Bloom with their editorial eye. But there was none to be found!

Elizabeth Bloom waited. The seconds dragged on. Then she said, "Let's remember that the writer is in this room. Let's help this individual out."

Finally, a hand went up. "I'm not sure about the line, 'It's been a hundred years,'" a woman in the front said. "I mean, the writer of this query seems to be claiming the fact that there hasn't been a popular golf fiction story in a hundred years is a *positive*. But to me, that seems like a negative. Like there's a reason there hasn't been successful golf fiction in the past hundred years."

Elizabeth Bloom raised a skeptical eyebrow to the room.

"That's what I was thinking," a man from the side said. "I think the writer should take that sentence out."

"They should take the whole paragraph out," another voice said. "I mean I'm not a golfer, but it's not like Weaver McCracken is a household name."

"Maybe it is to golfers," someone said.

"But is golf storytelling really a great tradition?" still another voice chimed in. "I mean, I think if it was, we non-golfers would have *at least* heard of it."

Another hand went up. "Can we talk about the first paragraph? The shattered window and the girl undressing. It seems like the writer is to trying a little *too* hard to stand out, to catch an agent's eye. I wonder, with an opening like this, if an agent doesn't see through it and just move on to the next query."

I could see where this was going. It was a critique session full of writers. So of course writers try to find things wrong with it. Like all good writing, my letter had provoked debate. There was no need to split hairs. I raised my hand.

"Yes, in the back," Elizabeth Bloom said.

"I think this letter is complete shit," I said with a straight face. "This writer should probably never write another word."

Heads turned. Jaws dropped. Sharp inhales sucked the air right out of the room. I kept my poker face for another moment. Hold, hold.

"Just kidding," I said with a grin. "It's mine. Thanks everyone for the feedback. I appreciate it."

The tension was cut. The air rushed back in, like balloons deflating. Palpable relief. Now they didn't have to come up with things to say. Elizabeth Bloom squinted at me. It was a look a chess player might throw when they are caught off guard by a brilliant move. She dealt mostly in young adult, otherwise I might have her and Ray Giese fighting over me.

"Let's move on," she said.

*

When the session was over, Elizabeth Bloom offered to read my query letter again, if I make revisions. Very gracious of her. She was giving off a vibe like a teacher when a student has been a little naughty but that the teacher appreciates it in a way.

I made my way out to the hall and glanced over my schedule for the day. The next hour I had a choice between Plot Like a Pro and Develop Deep Characters. I had ten minutes to make up my mind. I grabbed a seat on a bench and decided to do a little people watching.

That's when it hit me. Weaver McCracken was here. He could walk by at any moment. Suddenly my point of view shifted. This was no luxurious people-aquarium gazing affair— I was on the lookout.

How could I be bothered with plot or character development when Weaver McCracken might be around the next corner? I figured the best place to go was near the front of the hotel. That's where the registration was, as well as the coffee shop. Bathrooms, elevators. Lots of foot traffic.

I found a seat right in the center of the lobby, the perfect vantage point, and pulled out a copy of McCracken's breakthrough novel. The book that blew open the door of an entire genre, golf sci-fi. *The Dark Side of the Back Nine.* An instant classic.

I sat, debating whether to have him sign my copy, if it might make me seem like a fan and not a fellow writer, when I remembered the scratch out there in the parking lot. A steady flow of people swam by. The car could belong to any one of them. I imagined the person finding it, how it would ruin their day. The lobby became more and more crowded. I didn't want to give up my seat which, in addition to being comfortable, was the perfect vantage point.

But right is right. I realized my conscience would gnaw at me the rest of the day if I didn't go out there and leave a note. Which is what I did. I grabbed my bag and headed out to the parking garage. The SUV was still there. I left a handwritten note, apologizing and including my contact information.

No sooner had I tucked the paper under the windshield wiper, I felt a weight lift off my shoulders. I was ready now. I was ready to meet Weaver McCracken. I was ready to change my life.

Someone had ganked my spot. The publishing world is like that—leave a seat open, an opportunity, and it's gone in a flash. I found another seat on the fringe of the lobby. Not as comfortable, but still a good vantage point for an emerging writer on the verge of breaking in. The lobby sure was jammed. Writers, agents, publishers. The biz. A real buzz floated around. These were people that made a living on words, stories, ideas. You could feel the energy.

I surveyed the scene for a time. There was no sign of Weaver. I glanced at my watch and saw that the next sessions were starting. I had a choice between Edit Yourself Into Print and Write Effective Dialogue.

I started to scroll through the rest of the day. All these sessions, not one of them called, Meet Your Hero. So I stayed put.

The morning passed without a sighting. There was no sign of him at the complimentary luncheon, either. I roamed the ballroom with my tuna salad, just to make sure. I did spot Amy, the self-hug writer. She waved me over to an open seat, but I declined. I had to be sure Weaver wasn't lurking.

Then I realized: a writer like Weaver McCracken couldn't just walk into a complimentary lunch at a writers' conference and eat a ham sandwich. He would get mobbed. It made sense that he was lying low.

I tried a new strategy for the afternoon. Instead of staying fixed in one spot, I decided to roam. I dropped in on a panel session on hybrid publishing. I flitted into The Organized Writer. I drifted through genre spotlights: thrillers, romance, YA, memoir, mystery … I floated through it all.

And it paid off. I dipped out of a session called Relationships Are the Heart of Your Story, and lo, right in a hotel hallway, was Weaver McCracken. He was with his entourage. I saw Ray Giese. There were a handful of others. I guessed them to be his publicist, editor, assistants. All the roles a top writer needs filled.

He strolled along as if the hallway was the 18th fairway of a tournament, a tournament that had already been decided, a tournament he had won. He even wore golf attire, down to the shoes. The tan skin, perfect hair. He was like a ghost, unreal. But it was him. Weaver McCracken, in the flesh.

I took a deep breath and started in his direction, gaining on his leisurely stroll. This was it. I pulled out my manuscript. My thoughts raced. Do I call him Weaver? Or Mr. McCracken? Definitely Mr. McCracken. I had rehearsed this moment, but suddenly I couldn't recall my lines, the words that would steer our conversation to my story. He was twenty feet away, chatting with one of his people. My rehearsed lines came to me. *Mr. McCracken, it's an honor to finally meet you in person. You read my story,* The Pull Hook Wish. *Though I feel I already know you. If it's not too much to ask …*

This was it.

"Can I help you?"

A short man with a wide face and gray hair stood in my way. He had a bump on his cheek, like he had a golf ball in his mouth.

"I don't think so," I said. "I was just on my way to meet an author I admire."

"You mean Mr. McCracken," he said. He wore a mock turtleneck and a blazer.

"Yes."

"As a matter of security," the man said. I took a step, but he barred my way. The entourage was moving down the crowded hallway. "Mr. McCracken doesn't engage with the public."

"I'm not the public," I said. "I'm someone he has corresponded with." I pulled out my letter. "He's written to me. By hand. He's read my manuscript. I wanted to thank him. I've followed his advice and wanted to share the changes."

The man looked up at me, narrowing his eyes. "Are you, by any chance, the author of a story about hooks and wishes?"

"Yes," I said. "That's me. Sam Smith. *The Pull Hook Wish.* Mr. McCracken has commented directly on my story."

"I see," the man said. "We thought you might be here. My name is Bill Reid. I'm Mr. McCracken's publicist." He glanced down the hallway. Weaver's party had advanced around a corner.

"Nice to meet you," I said, starting to move. Bill Reid walked with me, angling me off with his short, quick strides so that I couldn't gain any ground.

"I can relay a message to Mr. McCracken that you're here," Bill Reid said. "Have you picked up a copy of his newest Red Course novel yet?"

Of course I had. *Dust Storm on the Red Course.* Another stroke of genius.

"Mr. McCracken will be signing copies of his book after his keynote address on Sunday," Bill Reid said. "Why don't you say hello then?"

"No … but see … listen," I said. "I'm more than just a fan. I've come so far and worked so hard on my story, with the help of Mr. McCracken. I was hoping to sit down with him and share my progress."

Bill Reid took two long strides and wheeled around in front of me.

"That won't be likely," he said.

I looked around him and saw Weaver and his people get into an elevator.

"But … I …"

"Please don't trouble Mr. McCracken at his paid events," Bill Reid said. He worked his tongue behind the golf ball bump in his cheek, like it needed an adjustment. "We take his security and privacy very seriously. I hope we won't have to involve the hotel security staff as well."

Bill Reid turned and walked off. When he got to the elevator, he turned back and threw a look at me. One of those *I mean it* looks.

There had to be some misunderstanding. Had someone else written a similar story, but taken their correspondence too far?

*

I decided to skip the panel with Weaver that night. I needed to regroup. Rethink my strategy. I headed home. In the morning,

I dredged myself from lurid dreams with snatching metal jaws and put on my suit, but skipped the yellow tie. Driving down to the conference, cruising along the highway, I realized that not wearing the tie was a sign: My belief in myself was eroding. It occurred to me that I skipped breakfast too.

Meeting Weaver McCracken was more important than ever.

The second morning of the conference was chock-full of workshops. I flitted amongst crammed hotel suites: Mastering the Sentence, Bring Your Fiction to Life, Adding Realistic Diversity, Respecting Your Reader, Silence Your Inner Critic. Weaver was nowhere to be seen. I staked out the lobby and the coffee bar, wandered corridors and hallways, monitored parking lots, popped into restrooms, watched elevators, even scoped the pool and fitness center. No Weaver.

It was around eleven o'clock when I started getting light-headed, dizzy. I still hadn't eaten anything. I headed across the street to a burrito joint. I thought I might pass out, so I focused on the tile floor in front of me. That's when I saw the bottom of a pair of khakis. I followed them up to a dry-fit, tucked in, blue striped golf shirt. My eyes moved up the neck, the perfect hair. It was him. Weaver McCracken was in front of me in line, at a burrito joint. This was so perfect. I waited for him to finish his order. I would just jump in, like I had rehearsed. *Mr. McCracken, it's me, Sam Smith, the author of* The Pull Hook Wish. He was paying with a credit card. *I want to thank you, to let you know how much you've inspired me.* He was ordering extra salsas, more green ones, then more red ones, the really spicy red ones. *I wouldn't be a writer without your work, I'm not even sure I would still be alive.* No—that was too much. The guy behind the register, oblivious to the greatness in front of him, handed over a soft drink. I watched this hand that had held me, figuratively, that had grabbed my imagination and walked onto fictional golf courses of glory and truth, fairways of hope and rough of despair. We had taken journeys together, learning so much about life. I watched his hand guide the straw right toward the target with precision accuracy. He took a sip. *Leave out the not being alive part. Focus on writing.* His food was ready. *Mr. McCracken, your writing has meant the world to me.* He was gathering his salsas, having an issue with a lid on one of the ramekins. It was one of the red salsas. Maybe work in a line about the red salsa, about his masterful use of red ink when the cyclops-pirates take over the clubhouse. I saw his fingers, the same fingers that had typed The Red Course trilogy, that had blasted golf fiction readers to Mars, an incredible ride, right in front of me, securing a lid—no, the lid won't fit. He decided not to bother. Of course not. He created a new genre of writing; he doesn't need lids on his ramekins. He was picking up his tray, turning around. *Mr. McCracken, you've shown me that art is possible.*

I stepped in front of him. It was one of those moments. You know it's real but it feels like a dream. He wasn't expecting me to move like I did. The soft drink toppled to the ground. Little ramekins joined the beverage, the ice made pattering sounds hitting the tile. Time stopped. In that instant, a light bulb flashed a comparison to McCracken's masterful descriptions of sand raining down on greens. A great sadness filled me, the feeling that I would never be able to tell him this, that I would never find the right words. That these lost, elusive words would join *The Pull Hook Wish* on the bottom of the sea. Time resumed.

He lurched forward, crunching the tray against my chest, to keep it from falling. I felt something cold and wet against my breast. His eyes, a look of surprise. His mouth, trying to shape words. He held up the tray, pressed it against me. Then he spoke.

"What the hell, man!"

"Oh, sorry, I thought you were someone else."

He let everything fall to the ground. I had red salsa smeared on my white shirt. He had the exact frame of Weaver McCracken, the same height and hair, but a completely different face, like a stunt double. "What are you, some kind of chuck wagon funny boy?" Then he turned around and said to the man behind the counter, "I'll need that order again."

*

After lunch I went back to the hotel and wandered around some more. I started to feel like one of McCracken's ghosts, endlessly meandering the same hole repeatedly. I found myself sitting in the front row of a session doing something that I do from time to time: sinking down and feeling sorry for myself. I know I shouldn't do it, but I do. I felt it rising up, the pity, and I let it climb, almost like a blanket that provides warmth and comfort, until it reached my chin, then I shook it off. Get off, I said to myself. I pulled out my notebook and decided to take some notes. It was a session titled The Science of Creativity.

I was shocked. Here was some academic, this woman with a ridiculous scarf and spiky haircut that made her look like a woodpecker, talking about creativity like it's a golf swing, like it has these specific, mechanical moves that are right and wrong. She went on with all these slides that crammed human imagination into dull, restrictive diagrams. I looked around and saw other writers taking it in, absorbing her words. It felt like someone explaining how to put on a straitjacket. Damage was being inflicted. Can you put the imagination of a Picasso, a Miles Davis, a Georgia O'Keefe, a Weaver McCracken into a diagram? Someone needed to say something, on behalf of the writers, so I did.

"I don't agree with you," I said.

"What?" the woodpecker woman responded, like I had hurled an egg at her.

"You don't put reins and a saddle on wild horses," I said.

Her lip curled. "Thank you, Mr. Jagger." She went back to her slide about finding creative minutes in a day. "For example," she said, looking at me with malice in her eyes. "Tell us something you have to do tomorrow."

"What?"

"Tell us something you have to do tomorrow, as an example for the group."

"Brush my teeth."

"Yes, how creative."

She went on with her slides, and I thought about all the conferences all over the country that this woman goes to, gets paid to attend, and the damage she inflicts, pecking at writers with her slides. Soon it was over, and I shuffled out with the rest. I thought somebody might come up to me with a comment like, "Can you believe her?" But nobody did. It was like all the other writers were hypnotized, in a trance.

I couldn't do it anymore. I couldn't sit in a workshop on backstory or attend a need-to-know before self-publishing. I went for a walk. Outside it was sunny, hot, and dry. The Santa Ana winds had picked up. There was a little river that trickled along behind the hotels, right across from a golf course. I figured I might as well go for a stroll to clear my head.

After about ten minutes I sat down on the edge of the stream and looked down into the water. I watched the water and let everything go. Pretty soon I started seeing people. I saw my older brother, the doctor, and his pregnant wife. I saw their life float down the stream like so many leaves. More kids. A new house. His successful career. All the birthday parties and events I would attend as the loser uncle.

I saw my other brother, the lawyer, and his fiancée, the wedding I would have to attend. I saw my parents, everyone lining up for a photograph, me banished to the edge.

I saw all my coworkers at the restaurant. I watched their lives float down the stream, perhaps finding a way out, perhaps not. Uncertain futures.

Then I saw myself. I really saw myself, maybe for the first time in my whole life, sitting on the edge of a stream with a manuscript I had spent years slaving over, that everything was riding on.

I watched the water gurgle on. I looked ahead to where it went. I saw the way it swirled around rocks, like lumps of vulnerability. I realized I could do the same thing, churn and eddy my way around my own vulnerabilities and get downstream. I saw myself there, in a place where I felt a sense of wellness. A place where I wasn't so anxious or sad or nervous all the time. A place where stories filled the air, where writers filled every café. It was right there, just beyond the riverbend.

I leaped up and rushed back. It was four thirty. There was a pitch session at five. Who knows? Weaver McCracken might even attend. I hustled on.

*

The hotel was ahead of me, but there, on the edge of the river, was the formidable figure of Ray Giese, talking on his cell phone. My luck was changing. Here was my chance.

I approached respectfully, getting close enough that he would see me, but not so close that I could overhear his conversation, likely some deal involving McCracken's works.

I stood there, waiting patiently. *I never had a chance to thank you for your astute feedback yesterday. I was wondering if you'd be willing …*

Out of nowhere a figure stepped in front of me. Bill Reid. It was like he came out of the reeds along the river. I grappled with a way to point out the irony of this when he spoke.

"Is there something I can help you with?"

"No," I said. "I noticed Mr. Giese here, and I wanted to thank him for his feedback on my manuscript."

"I can thank him for you," Bill said. He was wearing a different mock turtleneck and the golf ball lump in his cheek was a little red, maybe from the wind.

"No, see, there was a misunderstanding."

"Misunderstanding?"

"I was hoping Mr. Giese would read my revised beginning."

"Listen," Bill said, stepping toward me and looking up. He worked the golf ball in his cheek with his tongue. "I know who you are. We all know who you are. You need to stop harassing Mr. McCracken. He doesn't want to read any more of your story. He's a writer, not a developmental editor. You can find those online."

"Mr. McCracken and I have a running correspondence," I said.

Bill Reid laughed. "Oh please, that was just our intern having a little fun."

I didn't know what to say. I looked over at Ray Giese, using his hands to sort through the deal he was crafting. Could it be possible?

"Sorry, kid, but the world doesn't owe you any special favors. My advice to you is, Do what everyone else at this conference is doing: learn the craft. Now why don't you head on back inside and leave Mr. Giese to do the work of real writers?"

I was about to turn away, but no. I had done the work. I had revised.

"I've done the work," I said. "My revised beginning—"

"All right," Bill Reid said. "I thought it might come to this. Let me see it, kid. Let me see your revised manuscript."

I hesitated for a moment. It was my only copy, though I had backed it up in the cloud and on my hard drive. I handed it over.

"Did you revise the shirt part?" he said, flipping through the pages.

"I did. The significance of the tucked-in shirt was not apparent in the opening pages so I—"

"Just as I thought," he said with a guffaw. "You didn't revise it. It's moved back. Here it is on page eleven." He flipped the pages and counted to five. "Five pages about whether to tuck in a shirt." He closed my manuscript and smiled a tight smile that stretched over the lump in his cheek. "Listen, kid, nobody likes the rejection part of our business, but I believe it's better to hurt someone with the truth than to comfort them with lies. You are an amateur. Your writing exemplifies the term slush. There is no substance. An absurd, meandering plot. Paper-thin characters. I wasn't going to tell you this, but we all laugh at it. We pass it around and read it when we need comic relief. This might seem harsh, but I'm doing you a favor."

He tossed the manuscript into the little pond adjoining the river. The pages fluttered in the strong wind like an awkward swan landing.

"Start over. Go back to square one, kid," Bill Reid said. "If you really want it, you'll get there."

*

I walked in a daze back toward the hotel, not realizing I was going in through a service entrance.

"No puedes entrar aqui," a maid said to me, standing over her cart folding a towel.

"What?"

"You no enter here," she said again.

"Oh, I'm a writer," I said. I reached in my bag to pull out *The Pull Hook Wish*. "I'm here for the conference." Then I realized my manuscript was floating in the river. "I have a novel," I said.

She put down the folded towel and crossed her arms.

"It's about this golfer, he pulls his drive into a window and meets the love of his life."

She spoke again in Spanish, pointing and waving like I had to go around to the main entrance.

I pointed to the river. "It's floating in the river if you want to read it," I said.

I drove straight home. My phone was full of messages, everyone wanting to know how it had gone, but I didn't talk to anyone. I heated up a microwave lasagna, watched six episodes of *The Office*, and fell asleep on the couch.

I woke up the next morning with a realization. Bill Reid had an agenda. He was probably a wannabe writer himself, pretending to be a publicist, trying to make it on Weaver McCracken's coattails. It was obvious. He recognized my manuscript as a threat. Why else would he have been so aggressive?

I gave myself a hard look in the mirror. I remembered that vision around the riverbend, that place of wellness, beyond the curve. Who knows how close? Maybe it was today. Weaver McCracken was giving a keynote address about sports and fiction.

I put on my suit. My good white shirt still had a little pink salsa stain, but I covered it up with my yellow tie. I drove with the windows down and the radio on full blast. There was no traffic. I arrived a little early and walked out to the river beyond the hotel. There was my manuscript, floating in the middle of the pond. There were some rocks leading out, right near it.

I pulled off my socks and shoes and stepped out. A sliver of moon was setting in the west. It was like something in a Truman Capote story, obstacles in a path to self-realization. I could get there, one stone at a time.

And I did, except on the last rock I fell in. I didn't care. I pulled in my manuscript like I was rescuing a wounded bird, a bird that was ready to fly.

I didn't bother with the stones on the way back. I waded back to the shore. I stood there, drenched. It was another morning of Santa Ana conditions, hot and dry. I felt good, refreshed. And I had my manuscript.

I walked inside, grabbed a coffee and a roll, and got a seat in the front row for Weaver's address. Twenty minutes later, the room had filled up with writers of sports and fiction, eager to hear the words of a master.

He walked in right on time and stepped up to the podium like the first tee of a major, calm and confident. Bill Reid saw me, with my wet hair and soggy clothes, and did a little double take.

"People love sports," Weaver began. "We play them as children, and they carve a place deep within our hearts. In a few weeks, millions of people will gather to watch a football game."

After his introduction, I found I was so excited I couldn't listen. All my rehearsing came back to me. I would have a straight line to the podium when he finished. Nothing could stop me now.

Toward the end of his speech I hung on every word, waiting for the last, for my chance to leap forward, the chance of a lifetime.

His voice took on a concluding tone. "And this is where we must aim our pen," Weaver said, "a bull's-eye in our hearts, our deep love of sport."

People started clapping. I jumped up so fast my seat fell over. Bill Reid stood up, but it was too late. I was there, at the podium, next to Weaver McCracken.

"Mr. McCracken, my name is Sam Smith, the author of *The Pull Hook Wish*," I heard myself say in a bold, confident voice. "We've corresponded multiple times and I would just like to say it's an honor to meet you in person."

He crinkled his eyebrows and rubbed his chin. "Sam Smith … I know that name," he said.

"Yes sir, your feedback about my to-tuck-or-not-to-tuck opening was very insightful," I said.

A few people started to gather around; one of them was an organizer for the conference. I could tell because of the laminated nametag.

Weaver looked at me with keen, searching eyes. "Sam Smith. Where do I know that name from?" He kept rubbing his smooth, freshly shaven chin. Then it was like a light turned on. "Sam Smith! I know you. You hit my car on the first day of the conference. I got your note."

I felt my lips moving like a fish, opening and closing without sound.

"I appreciate your honesty," he said. "Not something you come across much anymore. Quite rare indeed these days."

The laminated name tag took another step forward. "Mr. McCracken, wonderful address. If you would follow me this way please."

"Wait."

They both looked at me, Weaver McCracken and the laminated name tag person.

"Wait," I repeated. "Mr. McCracken, I … um, see, I … I was so eager to talk to your agent, Mr. Giese, that I pulled in a little too sharp. Mr. Giese read the middle of my manuscript and, well, there was a little misunderstanding—"

"We'll get it straightened out," he said. "I have your information from the note." As he turned to go, he reached out and I shook his hand. "Pleasure meeting you, Mr. Smith. We'll be in touch. Thank you again for not just driving off."

Those words echoed in my head all the way home. *I have your information. We'll be in touch.*

THINGS WILL COME DOWN FROM THE SKY

1.

We were all on the driveway, about to go down the street.

"This is ridiculous," I said. "She can't just sit in her room all day."

Laura countered with, "She's been through a lot this week. Both her friends moved away."

Both her friends went away to college, which is what she should be doing. But Laura would have none of it. We started in on the same old argument when the helicopter came over the hill. It was moving fast. It hovered right over us for a moment, a police helicopter, drowning out Laura's voice. As it flew off, she shouted, "Do what you have to."

I went up the stairs and knocked on the door.

"Go away," my stepdaughter said.

"Can we talk?" I asked. I heard the helicopter off in the distance.

"No. You're not my father," she said for the thousandth time. "You can't make me do anything."

"You can't sit inside all day and do nothing," I said through the door.

"I'm working," she said.

Right, the novel. Since she ditched plans to enroll in community college, she announced that she wanted to be a writer. She's spent the past two months holed up in her room doing God knows what. This from a girl that barely passed senior English and spends all day on her phone. I've never seen her *reading*, much less writing. But apparently she does, though she doesn't share it with me or her mother or anyone else. I'd had enough. I stood in the hallway thinking when the sound of the helicopter came back.

"Everyone is going to the block party to celebrate the end of summer," I said.

We both heard the helicopter's voice making an announcement, which I couldn't understand on account of my step-daughter screaming to LEAVE HER THE FUCK ALONE. We'll see about that. We'll see, all right. I've had enough of her locked door and alleged novel. Just about enough.

2.

I got back down to the driveway. Laura acted like nothing had happened, like I hadn't even gone inside, like I had momentarily disappeared in a sprinkle of magic fairy dust. Daisy, our nine-year-old, was anxious. "What did the helicopter man say?" she asked.

"Nothing," Laura said. "Only that they are looking for a person."

"Why are they looking for a person?" Daisy asked. She had that worried look she gets and was breathing fast. "Is it a bad person?"

"We don't know," Laura said. Daisy was making our six-year-old Blake nervous. He was watching her and getting anxious too.

"Will the bad man try to kidnap me?" Daisy asked.

I looked over as Melody, our four-year-old, picked at a wad of gum on the street and put it in her mouth. "Icky," I said to Melody. She looked right at me, watched me for a moment, and then put more gum in her mouth.

"No," I said, walking over to her and picking her up. "Icky. Bad."

"Don't worry," Laura said to Daisy. "If you see the bad man and we're not with you, if he tries to take you, remember what you learned in your self-defense class. Go chihuahua crazy."

"What's chihuahua crazy?" Blake asked. He was getting worried. The helicopter disappeared beyond the hill. Its blades reverberated in our neighborhood, which is like a big fishbowl.

"Did you grab the cooler with the popsicles?" Laura asked, as if I hadn't even gone inside at all, as if her future-less daughter, locked inside her room for yet another day, wasn't even an issue. The popsicles were the urgent issue. I went inside to get them, slamming the door. When I came back, Laura acted like everything was hunky-dory. "I'll guess I'll get the cooler, too," I said out loud, hearing my voice echo a little in the garage.

3.

We walked down the street toward the block party. I was carrying the cooler with the popsicles. I tried to make Daisy carry it, but she was all worried about the helicopter.

"It's fine," Laura said. "Let's just go."

So we did.

Kids were everywhere. A big celebration. The end of summer. One last hurrah. There was a big red and blue jumpy rollicking with kids, and tables crammed with snacks and treats. It was bright, hot, and sunny, the heat pulsing off the concrete.

Daisy and Blake dashed off, joining a massive boys vs. girls water fight. I handed Laura the popsicles. With Melody on her hip, she took them over to the snack table, right next to a shade structure filled with teenagers, sitting in a circle, all on their phones. All the husbands were on the corner, in a little circle, in front of Louie's yard. Water was gushing from his irrigation system. Mitchell was a little ways away. I asked him what it was all about.

"Louie's got a burst pipe," Mitchell said. I joined the circle and gave everyone fist bumps. We all stood around and talked about what Louie should do. It was agreed upon that Louie should dig up the cracked pipe, since Andrew had some PVC pipe that he could use to replace it. The same thing had happened to Paul last month.

Daisy came running over.

"Did you see the bad man?" she whispered.

"No, don't worry about that," I said. "You have nothing to worry about."

I asked Mitchell if he had heard the helicopter fly overhead. "What?" He was going to get a shovel to help dig. The water streamed into the gutter and flowed down the street. I saw Melody downstream, playing in it. I saw her bend down and take a sip.

"Ick!" I shouted. "Don't drink. Icky."

I asked Bill if he heard the helicopter searching for someone. "Oh, that," Bill said. "Yeah, we heard that."

All the men dispersed, off to get tools for the project. Shovels, pickaxes, PVC pipes, other instruments of irrigation.

"This is going to be a big job," Bill said. "I'm going to grab my jackhammer." He walked off.

"I've some extra glue, I think," I said and walked over to Laura. An orange blob sailed right past my head. I ducked just in time, the water balloon splashing on the concrete. A flock of drenched girls in swimsuits surged past me, screaming.

Laura and all the other moms were talking about the helicopter. It was all over the internet. Facebook. Twitter. Instagram. A neighborhood website called "The Ladies of Luminara Hills." The cops were searching for someone, all right.

"Should we take the party inside?" Diana asked.

Everyone looked at the jammed street. I could see their faces trying to imagine taking it inside.

"Well, that's not happening," Nicole said, and everyone laughed.

I wanted to tell Laura that I was headed back, that I was going to grab some glue for Louie's irrigation project, but I couldn't get a word in. Plus, Melody was clinging to her neck, whimpering about something. I watched her wipe snot on Laura's shirt and then lick it. I gave her a frowny-face headshake. The wives were all talking about keeping an extra eye out, forming a perimeter, stationing a few parents down in the cul-de-sac, near the fence by the ravine.

"What did this person even do?" Allie asked.

Nobody seemed to know. One tweet said a suspected arsonist. The Ladies of Luminara said attempted kidnapping. Christine said that her sister's friend heard it was breaking and entering. Everyone was looking at their phones, scanning the horizon.

I tapped Laura on the shoulder. "I'm going to get some glue," I said. She nodded the nod she uses when she doesn't care what I'm saying, when she wants me to go away.

4.

I walked off back toward our house. It felt good to get away from the noise and frenzy. I looked back and marveled at it all. Then I turned and continued walking, looking at the blue sky, counting the hours until the sun would go down, adding another two hours for the pizza and movie, then likely another hour of overtired tears until finally, we could put everyone down and crash. One moment at a time, I told myself.

I've been working on my mindfulness, trying to live in the present. I looked at all the trees as I walked along, the dappled sunlight filtering through. I noticed the branches swaying in the breeze. I saw a dove dart between two houses and wondered if a hawk was nearby. There was no sign of the helicopter.

Down at the corner, a car turned onto the street, driving fast. I could see it was Carol in her BMW with her adopted teenage daughter Eun-woo. Carol was overprotective of Eun-woo and didn't let her out much. She was fifteen, maybe sixteen, just reaching that age.

Carol was driving even faster than usual, pulling into her driveway a few houses down from ours. I'm quite friendly with Carol. We chat mostly about education, how Eun-woo is adapting to her American high school. Carol is a retired teacher. I work in human resources for a school district. We always have something to talk about.

I expected to discuss Eun-woo's looming sophomore year, but Carol got right out of her car, shouted something at Eun-woo, and made a beeline to her door, scrambling in her purse for her keys. "Get inside, now," she said. Before slamming the door, she turned and saw me, but didn't wave or smile or anything. I heard the door bolt.

5.

I found the glue in the garage and set it on the counter. I also grabbed my small axe, which I remember Mark saying they might need to cut tree roots. I stood in the kitchen and listened. Not a sound. I walked over to the stairs. Still nothing. Totally quiet. I thought I could hear the helicopter, far off, but maybe it was my imagination.

You're cruising for a rude awakening, I wanted to shout to my stepdaughter. Life is going to rip her apart. How could Laura not see this? She didn't need time or extra love or space or all the nonsense Laura keeps talking about. She needed a swift kick in the pants. A firm talking to. A job.

I went up the stairs and knocked softly with the blunt end of the axe. Nothing.

"Everyone is down the street," I said.

I waited.

"Not because I say so," I said, "or that I'm your father or any of that. But think of your brother and sister. Next summer you might be busy: school, work, whatever you decide. This could be your last summer with them. The least you could do is make an appearance for dinner, to show that you care."

I stood and waited again.

Finally, quiet as a mouse: "When I finish this chapter I'll come," she said.

I gripped the handle of the axe and grinded my teeth. I swallowed hard, then I was hacking away, chopping like a madman, wood flying, smashing the door that she thinks she can hide behind forever, that life won't eventually come for her, that she can say, my novel, and we'll feed her and house her forever. That she won't have to lift a finger.

I took a deep breath. Mindfulness. I felt the smooth wood of the door, ran my finger along the axe. I noticed the way the grains flowed on the handle, rubbed them with my thumb. I looked at a square of sunshine coming through the window, one corner still on the floor, the rest starting to climb the hallway wall. I watched specks of dust floating in the shaft of light. I looked at our family picture. Everyone smiling. Except Miranda. I snorted a small laugh. Probably too busy thinking about her novel.

"Things are going to change around here," I said. I tapped the door with the handle of the axe again. "I'll take this door right off. You'll see. You want to be treated like an adult. Careful what you wish for."

6.

I grabbed the glue and went out through the garage, right into Shauna, walking her golden retriever, Shiloh. We bump into her practically every day, usually right when we are trying to leave. She's a sweetheart, but a real talker.

"Hi, Shauna," I said.

"Can you believe it?"

"What?"

"This helicopter," she said. "An escaped felon, running loose in Luminara Hills. It's not enough that we have teenagers running around keying cars and destroying property. Now we have to fear for our lives. I guess there's no safety anywhere."

"Where did you hear all that?"

"It's everywhere. It's on the news. There's a video of him running across Canyon Road, right down into the ravine. I almost didn't come out, but I wanted to get Shiloh a walk before night falls. Then who knows? Thankfully we have Shiloh to keep watch."

Shiloh, quite possibly the oldest and gentlest dog alive, walks more than most people. His tongue hung down as he panted in the shade.

"Yeah, well, the police will handle it," I said.

"You carrying that for protection?"

"What? Oh, the axe. No. Louie has a problem with his irrigation. This is for the roots. To help cut the roots."

She looked at me from behind her enormous sunglasses. She always wore the same thing— same hat, sunglasses and yoga pants. "Well, probably not a bad thing to have on you," she said. "Be careful. This person is a real wacko."

"What did he do?"

"It doesn't matter. Something horrible. Something that has the police chasing him in a helicopter."

A man walking a big gray wolf-looking husky approached on the other side of the street. Shiloh stood up and started barking. The other dog barked back; its owner gripped the leash tighter and moved in between the dog and the street.

"Shhh," Shauna said. "Quiet Shiloh." She gave a tug on the leash.

The dog walker across the street sped up to a brisk pace.

"He's anxious," she said to me in a low voice. "It's the same breed that attacked him."

I nodded, looking at the way a thin crack snaked across a block of sidewalk.

"Shhh … not all dogs are bad," she baby-talked to Shiloh, still tense and barking. "It's the same breed," she repeated, pointing with her head at the dog moving along down the street. She started telling the story about how a big husky that still lives in the neighborhood attacked Shiloh when he was a puppy. This might have been the tenth time I had heard it. She finished with her usual closing: "Shiloh's a lover, not a fighter."

I nodded, watching the branches sway in the wind.

"You heard about when that monster bit a kid, right?"

"Sure," I said. It was a big deal, about a year ago. Sawyer, one of the boys in Daisy's class, got bit on the leg. It really freaked out Daisy—she wouldn't go near a dog for a month.

"They had to call animal services," Shauna said, Shiloh settling back into the shade as the other dog turned a corner. "They ordered the guy not to use retractable leashes anymore, but did this buffoon listen? No. He still walks that beast around with these absurd contraptions that wouldn't restrain a kitten, much less that monster."

I nodded, watching a leaf flutter.

"Can you imagine?" Shauna asked. "That something could come out of nowhere and attack you."

"Scary … well, I better get a move on," I said, waving good-bye with the axe.

7.

I walked back, carrying the axe and the glue. I breathed slow and easy, noticing the shadows starting to creep toward the east. Pandemonium romped around the corner, but here it was quiet and peaceful. I walked past Carol's house and thought maybe I saw her peek out from behind a curtain. Or maybe it was her cat.

I got back to the party, in full swing. The water balloon fight was over. All the kids were eating popsicles and ice cream on the curb. The men were all back with their tools, working.

"Didn't you get my text?" Laura said. Melody was on her hip, crying into her neck about wanting a purple popsicle.

"What?"

"I asked you to bring the swimsuits," Laura said. "Melody, you said you wanted a red popsicle. So that's what you get."

"No!" Melody screamed and threw the red popsicle on the ground.

"I didn't see your text," I said.

"That's *your* popsicle," Laura said to Melody. "You're not getting another one." Then to me: "Everyone is going swimming in Lia's pool." Melody was wailing, really letting loose.

"Do you want me to go back?"

"Yes."

"Are the adults going swimming?" I asked, but she didn't answer. Melody was screaming in her ear.

8.

I went over by all the guys digging and working. Tools and pipes were strewn about Louie's driveway and sidewalk. There were piles of dirt and mud. They had only managed to partially shut the water off. It was still gurgling and occasionally a spurt flew up. Louie was in the middle of it all, in his yard, on his phone.

"The extension cord's in," Paul called from the garage. "You're all set."

The orange extension cord led over to Kenny standing in a hole with a jackhammer. He started it up.

"Here's some extra glue," I shouted to Mitchell. He was sawing off some PVC pipe. He didn't hear me. I set the glue down on his work bench and waved. He looked up and nodded.

I walked back, away from the sound of the jackhammer. I rounded the corner of the cul-de-sac and thought I heard the helicopter again, though it might have been the noise from the jackhammer bouncing off the hillsides.

At least I was getting my steps in. I calculated that I had to be over five thousand, halfway to my daily goal. I took deep breaths and reminded myself to drink a glass of water. I held my expanded diaphragm. A crow floated by. The sunlight glinted off his back.

I went through the garage and into the kitchen. Miranda was standing at the counter like a ghost, scrolling on her phone, eating cheese and crackers. That's all she eats—she's rail thin. I swear she has an eating disorder. I swear she's on drugs. I got a glass of water and gulped it down.

"You sure you don't need a jacket?" I asked. "I can get the winter coats down from storage."

She was wearing, as always, a thick hooded sweatshirt and baggy jeans. What was new was her hair. She had dyed it black and wore the bangs over her eyes. It was like an extension of the black hoodie, like a visor that came down.

"I got stuck," she said in the soft voice she always uses with me. "I decided to take a break." She's either screaming at me or using that soft mouse voice. She can't talk to me in a normal voice. She can't talk to adults.

"Put on a swimsuit," I said. "Everyone's going swimming."

She smiled and stuffed a cracker with cheese in her face, mumbling something.

"What?" I barked. "I can't hear you with food in your mouth."

She swallowed and took a gulp of ice water. The food I buy. Water I pay for.

"I have an awards ceremony," she said. "I have to be back in an hour."

"Is that so?" I said.

She nodded and I waited. No clue that it was her turn to talk. A writer with communication skills lacking. I used my hands to show her that she needed to go on.

"A competition I entered," she said. "At the library. Short stories. I received an email this morning that the awards ceremony is this afternoon."

"An awards ceremony? As in, you've won an award?"

Laura texted me. I looked down at my phone.

Don't forget towels

"I don't know," Miranda said.

"Did they invite everyone that entered, or only the winners?"

"I'm not sure. It's not until later. I thought I would come down and say hi to Blake and Daisy. Like you asked."

"Well, all right," I said. "I'll grab their suits and we'll head down. You'll be back in plenty of time for your ceremony."

I was running my hand along the blade of the axe. I didn't realize that I was doing it and almost cut myself. That's what she does to me. I lose my mental awareness in her games. Awards ceremony. I set the axe down and went up the stairs for the swimsuits.

I was rifling through Blake's abomination of a drawer when Laura called.

"I know," I said. "I'll bring towels."

"Also," she said, "can you run to the store?"

"For what?" I could hear the party, the jackhammer. She was practically shouting at me; it was crazy loud.

"They didn't order any gluten-free pizza for Blake."

"I can't find his swimsuit," I said. "His room is a disaster." I chucked an armful of pajamas into the air.

"Check the dryer," Laura said. "I think his green one is in the dryer."

I could hear Melody asking for another bag of chips.

"Never mind," I said. "I found his blue one, on the bottom of his pajama drawer."

"No more chips," Laura said to Melody. Then to me: "Check the dryer anyway for his green one, that has the shirt. It's so sunny."

I could hear Melody whining for another bag of chips, the party, the jackhammer.

"All right," I said. "I'll check the dryer."

"Fine," Laura said. "But that's your last bag. Oh, and can you grab ice? The cooler is running low and all the ice cream is melting."

"One gluten-free pizza and a bag of ice," I said. "Do you want me to drop off the swimsuits and towels on my way?"

She didn't hear me. Katy Perry blared in the background.

I grabbed Daisy's suit and some towels and went back downstairs. I found Blake's in the dryer and poked my head into the kitchen. "I've got to run to the store," I said to Miranda, staring down at her phone. The cutting board, the cheese, the crackers all splayed out on the counter. "Will you take these swimsuits and towels down to your brother and sister?"

"I can go with you to the store," Miranda said.

"What about your awards ceremony?" I said. "Will you be back in time?"

"Sure," she said. "There's plenty of time."

"Whatever you say," I said, grabbing my keys.

9.

We walked outside, smack into Shauna and Shiloh, on their return trip. Miranda went straight over to Shiloh. She's better with animals than people.

"I wouldn't go out, dressed like that," Shauna said. "Unless you're trying to be funny."

"What?" I asked. Then I realized she was talking to me. "Why?"

"Aren't you following the news?" Shauna said. "They say the escaped felon has changed out of his orange prison clothes and is now dressed in a green shirt and baseball cap. Medium height and medium build. You're a dead ringer."

I heard the echoes along the hillsides, but it sounded more like a jackhammer to me. Miranda was speaking gibberish to Shiloh and rubbing behind his ears.

"Oh, nonsense," I said. I threw the towels, the swimsuits, and the axe in the backseat.

"Be careful," she said. "They're saying dead or alive. A real lunatic. They say he's wanted for arson and murder. He's a kidnapper, a killer, and an arsonist to boot. He's liable to do anything."

"Well, we're … running to the store," I said. "It's fine."

"That's the last place I'd go," she said. "This psycho might seek out a crowd, start shooting up the store."

"I'm sure the police have it under control," I said. "C'mon, Miranda. Let's go. The kids want to get into the pool, and you have your awards ceremony."

That was a mistake. Shauna has to know everything, even if she's running for her life.

"A short story," Miranda said, more to Shiloh than to Shauna.

"What's it about?"

"Sci-fi," Miranda said. "It's about an alien."

"Good for you," Shauna said. "So few people do anything creative anymore. I hope you win!"

We coasted in silence down the hill to the store. There wasn't any of the usual traffic.

"I guess everyone is out enjoying summer, while they still can," I said.

10.

Which was partly true. Everyone that wasn't at a party or a barbecue was at the grocery store. It was a madhouse. I told Miranda to get in line for the self-checkout and went for the pizza and the ice.

I met her in line. We stood there and inched along. Finally, I said, "I didn't know you wrote science fiction."

She managed a "yeah."

We stood there and the line hardly moved.

"So what happens to the alien?" I asked. "In your story."

"They don't know that they're aliens," she said. "They've been brainwashed by the government. Their memories have been wiped clean. Their families come to save them, but they don't know that the spaceships in the sky are their families, so they run to the government for help, without realizing that they are running away from their families."

"They? There is more than one?"

"The alien is both genders at the same time," she said.

"Oh, right, that's not confusing," I said.

I could tell that wounded her a little.

"Don't pay attention to me," I said. "I don't know anything. I hope you win. It's a good premise for a story."

"Thanks," she said, and smiled at me for the first time in what felt like years.

A woman at the front was causing a stir. She was getting charged for organic avocados, but her avocados weren't organic.

"Oy, jeez," I said.

That's when Miranda told me about her novel. It's about the same alien family. She said she took a break because she doesn't know how to end it. The aliens get their progeny back, but they don't know how to love them, and they don't know how to love their alien family in return. They don't know how to undo the government brainwashing.

The cashier pointed out to the woman that the avocados were indeed organic. They had to send someone for non-organic avocados. At another machine, a man was trying to buy this seltzer drink that he claimed was non-alcoholic. The manager had to explain that since it did have a low percentage of alcohol, it would need to be purchased at one of the registers. The customer was making a stink about it.

"So they go back to Earth," Miranda said. "To undo the brainwashing. They go to this secret base in the middle of the desert and they gets their memory back."

The ice I was holding dripped on the floor. The woman thought the non-organic avocados were too hard. The manager finally checked out the dude with the seltzer drink. Everyone in line was grumbling and glancing at each other. This was taking forever.

"But my character suffers a personality crisis and goes off into the middle of the desert to wander," Miranda went on. "They can't decide whether to live on Earth or go with these aliens that claim to be their family. I've left them dangling and don't know how to resolve it."

"I'm sure you'll manage," I said. "We might not make your awards ceremony at this rate."

11.

The wait felt like an eternity, but we finally made it out of the store. We walked to the car. I was putting the items into the trunk when suddenly I felt a gush of wind and a blast of sound. The helicopter roared above me.

"PUT YOUR HANDS ON TOP OF YOUR HEAD AND GET DOWN ON THE GROUND," a voice called from the sky.

"Oh, brother," I said. Miranda was already in the passenger seat. "Hey, listen," I called up to her. "Take the keys," I said and threw them to her. "The helicopter thinks I'm some criminal. I'm going to straighten this out. You head back."

"No," she said. "I'm staying with you."

The helicopter repeated the demand.

"Nonsense," I said.

The avocado woman was standing there, watching. "Can I help you?" I said to her. She got in her car. The helicopter blew up dust and trash. I watched a plastic bag whirl in a vortex of air.

"Listen, Miranda, take the pizza and ice and swimsuits to the party," I said. "This is one big misunderstanding. Besides, you have your awards ceremony."

"What if they arrest you?"

"They're not going to arrest me," I said. "That's foolish."

"GET ON THE GROUND NOW!"

"C'mon, let's go," Miranda said. Then she was out of the car, with the suits and the towels and the axe. "I know this secret tunnel behind the store." And she took off.

"Miranda, come back. Don't give them a reason—"

Then I was following her, running with the pizza and the ice. The helicopter was right above me, loud as hell, the sound bouncing off the concrete.

12.

I followed her around the corner, into an alley, down some stairs, along a dirt path, through some trees, and across a ditch that was covered with weeds. She hacked away with the axe and, sure enough, she was right; there was an irrigation tunnel. We could hear the helicopter close by, but we couldn't see it.

"Miranda stop," I called out. We heard the helicopter's amplified garble muffled by the trees. "Listen. This is a misunderstanding. Running is not the solution."

"Didn't you hear Shauna?" she said. "They're going to kill you. You're dressed the same as the crazy person. You've got to run."

I held up the shopping bags. "I have pizza and ice. Obviously I'm not a murderer."

She took my hand and pulled me toward the tunnel. I peered into its darkness, could feel the cool damp air. I resisted her tug.

"Miranda. No one is going to get shot."

"Here, take my sweatshirt," she said. She pulled off her hoodie, displacing the bangs that covered her eyes. Her neck was slender like a bird's. I looked into her dark eyes.

"Your awards ceremony," I said. "You need to get back."

"Dad," she said. "Please."

The helicopter repeated its garbled message above the trees. One moment it sounded close, the next far away. There was an echo off buildings, hills.

"Fine," I said. "Fine. But it's really not necessary." I put on the sweatshirt.

"Take this," she said, offering me the axe. "Follow the tunnel. It leads to the bike path. The one we used to ride together."

She took the pizza and ice. Sweat dripped into my eyes. My breath was all over the place. The sound was getting closer. We stepped into the tunnel. I was about to go, but something held me back.

A big gust of wind whooshed down. Was it from the helicopter? Was it getting lower? The tunnel distorted all sound.

Suddenly, she was hugging me and crying. We stood and held each other. Something disturbed the trees. Bullets? Were they firing at us?

"Listen," I said into her ear. "Someday, some helicopter is going to appear in your sky. I mean, it won't be like this. It won't be an actual helicopter, but you know what I mean. Something will appear in your sky and come down on you. It will appear and say that you are something you are not. In my case, it's a kidnapping arsonist-murderer … but in yours, it could be anything. Anything at all. But don't listen to it. Don't let it take you, make you into something you're not. Now run. Blake is probably starving. Get him his pizza." She turned to go. I watched her walk out of the tunnel.

"And Miranda," I called out. Her head poked into view. "Good luck at your awards ceremony!"

13.

TWENTY-SIX YEARS LATER

"How did I even get here?" Miranda asked herself, sitting outside the entrance of the Rincon Mountain Visitor Center, watching the rising sun poke through the clouds and spread rays of light across the desert world. She looked down at her name on the Saguaro National Park Ranger badge, ran her thumb over the letters.

Of course, she knew exactly how she got there. Community college for an associate's degree. Transfer to a state school. BA in English. The MFA applications that came up short. The job she took teaching middle school English. That was when it dried up, she thought. That's when her habit of writing ceased. Always too tired. Never in the mood. No new ideas. Don't force it, she remembered telling herself. Keep reading and the ideas will come. But they didn't.

She married her first serious boyfriend out of school, an accountant. He was good with numbers, smart. It felt safe, a good move, one her mother would approve of. But deep down it was never right. They both got terrible food poisoning on their honeymoon, and that seemed to set the tone for their marriage. Plus, he was allergic to everything. After a few years, it was almost like he was allergic to her.

The divorce was quick, efficient, business-like, as was everything he did. She decided to take the summer to travel and flew to Spain.

They met in a hostel in Barcelona. She fell for him hard and believed, for the first time, in love at first sight. They traveled for three weeks together. He said he worked in sales, some type of medical supplies. He said he could work from anywhere and moved to California for her.

That's when her writing flared up, briefly, intensely, like a flame. She wrote mad love poems into the night. Her mind wouldn't, couldn't shut down. Everywhere she went, everything she saw and did, every person she watched, it all had new meanings and connections. She wrote and wrote and wrote.

The flame went out as suddenly as it had come back to life, like wind to a candle. She accidently saw his email. A letter from his wife. He said that he was getting divorced, that it was taking forever. But he had lied to her, and it unraveled from there.

The seed of doubt had been planted. It grew when he would never show her his work, was vague about its details. Once he said he was working but she saw he was playing solitaire.

He always deleted the browsing history on his computer. She noticed his pop-up ads were all for online poker sites.

Looking back, it amazed her how blind she had been. How her own eyes had refused to believe. How even her own voice had tried to convince her to believe in his lies. Yes, she had loved him. But now, looking and thinking back, with her head and not her heart, what she really loved was how he had re-connected her to this mysterious source of her stories and writing, re-opened her imagination to the possibility of being a writer. She might have stayed with him if his deceit was only about his marriage and his career. If not for his drinking, like water on growing weeds.

When he had arrived in California, they had a big weekend of drinking and celebrating. But it became clear that his drinking wasn't just on the weekends and special occasions. He had cocktails and beers with lunch, Bloody Mary's in the mornings, even on the weekdays. Also, his drunkenness wasn't so fun or carefree anymore. She confronted him one night and it turned violent. He smacked her. She had to cover her black eye with makeup before school the next morning. From there it was a rollercoaster: steep drops of violence and abuse, slow and steady climbs back to something like normalcy, but then the drop again, the loop, the violence. He had been abused by his father. She loved him so deeply, so desperately. She wanted to save him, to fix him.

She didn't want to lose that feeling he gave her, that she had something to say.

Then she was pregnant. Then she was on the floor, curled into a ball, while he kicked her, kicked the baby. That night, while she was lying on the bedroom floor, he killed the life inside her. That's when she looked up and saw the framed certificate on the wall: Honorable Mention for Short Fiction from the Escondido Public Library.

After the procedure, she left California for Arizona. She decided to work as a park ranger, once again taking classes at a community college. A fresh start. A new land. The outdoors. A place to clear her head and get back to writing.

Every time she picked up a pen or opened her computer, all the stories in her mind were like a hissing rattlesnake. Don't get too close. She couldn't get near it, couldn't untangle it, much less try to write about it. That was eight years ago.

Sometimes out of nowhere a voice inside her would shout: YOU ARE NOT SOMEONE THAT LIES DOWN AND LET'S LIFE TRAMPLE YOU. YOU ARE AN OBSERVER, YOU HAVE POWERS, YOU ARE A WRITER. WAKE UP!

She walked into the lobby, listening to the movie in the theater wrapping up. The field trip from the local elementary school filed out into the lobby and she made her speech, the same one she'd been making for the last five years. After reminding everyone about water and sunscreen and wearing a hat, she led the group out of the lobby and down a path into the desert.

The first stop on the tour was a giant saguaro cactus towering over forty feet in the air. Miranda told her group of young naturalists, "The giant saguaro cacti represent the delicate balance between water, life, and the aridity of the desert."

Though it was just past eight in the morning, the heat of the coming summer day could already be felt.

She could do this tour in her sleep, she'd done it so many times. A keystone species. Storage of over two hundred gallons. Photosynthesis at night. Deep taproot, shallow root system. A dependence on nurse trees.

She heard herself say the final line before questions, the line she had said so many times.

"Saguaro cacti depend on nurse trees for propagation," she said. "And if global warming reduces the number of nurse trees, we will see a corresponding drop in this majestic plant, the universal symbol of the American West."

Then she heard a sound she hadn't heard in a long time, though she instantly recognized the approaching hum.

"Down!" she cried. "Get down! Bee swarm!"

She hit the ground and covered one of the nearby students as the bees descended. As she felt the first of what would be almost three hundred stings, she heard the voice of her first stepfather, a voice she hadn't heard or thought of in years, long obscured by the voices of other men: another stepfather, then a handful of successive boyfriends. But she heard his voice clearly, over the din of angry, swarming insects.

"Someday, something will come down from the sky."

SIDE MIRRORS

I don't remember when it started, exactly. I knew at the time that something had happened, but whatever it was was vague and slipped away before I even knew what hit me. A few weeks of muddled time went by, I think, before it happened again. Gradually it started happening more and more until, finally, the realization dawned on me, like a break in the clouds, a bright ray of sunshine. I almost rear-ended a truck in front of me. Red taillights flashed like an angry insect—I stopped just in time, my heart thudding in my chest, and I knew what had happened, what had been happening.

I'll tell you all about it, even if you don't believe me. In a way, it makes sense that you won't—can't—believe. It fits with all of it. Just like me on all those drives home when it first started. Doubt is a powerful thing, when you think about it.

Here's what it is: I acquired a strange power. I guess you could call it supernatural or paranormal or something like that. I don't really know how to classify it. I'm not sure how or when or why, but I acquired it, all right.

This is how I developed it. I commute home on the snarling freeways of southern California. Frequently, I'm inching along. Imagine another car, in front of me by a car's length in a lane next to me, inching along at the same speed, one or two miles an hour, on and off the brake. When I get in sync with a car like that, just behind but parallel, if you will, in the universe, I'm always curious about the person driving next to me. I see them, stark and clear, framed in their side mirror. I wonder about them. What kind of life do they have? Are they happy? Have they suffered anything truly heartbreaking? What do they want out of life? That kind of stuff. Sometimes my mind turns morbid. Here we are, both driving on this highway at this moment in time, but two thousand years from now we'll both be dead. Where will this body, this *stranger*, be buried? I know it's dark, but it's how I think.

Then, on that particular day when the realization hit me, I found that if I stared hard into their side mirror and concentrated on their reflection, it would happen. (The earlier incidents happened more or less by accident, but I got better at it. I guess I trained myself.) I was able to steal the person's thoughts. But not just *any* thoughts. If the person was listening to the radio, or singing a song, or thinking about work or what to buy for dinner or their plans for the weekend or anything mundane or superficial, then I wouldn't be able to take it. I would hear those thoughts, like fuzz on the radio or random background static—grocery lists, to-do lists, the monotonous humdrum— but I wouldn't be able to take them. It was only when their thoughts would stray, far in the distance, like an island off the coast. Then they were ripe for the picking, like the old saying: candy from a baby. And I noticed another thing. They always involved longing or a desire of some kind. Like something that didn't happen a long time ago. Or something that might happen tomorrow, but never does. Those kinds of thoughts. I found that when I stared at the side mirror as we eased along, if we were in sync long enough and the longing reached a threshold of intensity, then it was as simple as picking an apple from a tree. They more or less popped right off, and I had them.

The first time I did it consciously, the traffic was a real bitch. There was a significant pileup ahead, and together we all crawled along. The sun was setting into the ocean. Sure, it's beautiful, but it's more of a tease when you see it from a traffic jam and your body is tired and tense. There's this beauty that you can glance at but never have the time to admire. So why strain?

I was listening to an audio book, but it was putting me to sleep. Not sure if it was the writing or me, but I felt like the story was just meandering and not getting anywhere. My eyes were getting heavy, so I shut it off and rolled down the windows. I remember it was a brutally hot and dry day. The heat rose in waves off the pavement, but it mingled with a cool breeze that blew in from the ocean. Anyway, I was right next to this lady in a fancy SUV. Her enormous car had these immense side mirrors. One practically reached into my passenger's window. She had a nice profile. Probably in her mid-forties, but still attractive. Her hair was long and blond. Enormous sunglasses concealed her eyes. I was just looking, sort of admiring her profile in that side mirror, wondering about her life and her husband and her kids, when it jumped out at me. Her desire. She had had a true love once. Very early in life. But he died. A tragic death. I couldn't see him clearly, or how he died. But I felt her longing to be with him again. It was like *she* was seeing him, right through her windshield. Like he was there every day of her life, and it was starting to be too much. The whole thing floated right over to me.

The traffic staggered along. It was brutal, but suddenly I wasn't tired. I had this new thing to examine, to feel. In a way, it was quite lovely, though sad. She loved him so deeply. That early, young love, when anything is possible. It's thrilling. It was nice to feel that again. I had almost forgotten what it was like. I rolled along and held it, examined it like a small child might look closely at an interesting rock they found.

Finally, I made it past the accident causing the snarl, made my way north up the highway, then to the off-ramp. I hit every red light on the side roads, and pulled into my driveway to, well, a house on fire, so to speak. My wife was exhausted and had work to do. Our toddler had a fresh cold. The older one needed help with her homework. Even the cat was in a foul mood. I made dinner, did the dishes, helped with homework, got everyone to bed, and even managed a load of laundry. Normally I would drag myself through an evening like that with a heavy heart, a dazed expression of fatigue. Sort of like a mask. But on this night, I had a new source of energy.

At first, I wasn't sure what to do with it, but I realized I had to put it away, store it somewhere. You can't just walk around with a thing like that in your pocket. I opened up the crawl space in the attic and found a way to store it. It felt good, like it was secure and available if I should need it again.

Well, there are two things you don't need to predict in southern California: sunshine and traffic. That week, the traffic was as bad as ever. I found myself crawling along next to vehicles, and it was like these things were begging me to take them, to look into the side mirror and get them as far away as possible, as fast as possible. I took home lost dreams, forbidden loves and desires, broken hearts, tantalizing hopes … you name it. I pulled off the highway each day and always seemed to have a new one.

It was like fishing in a lake crawling with bass and having just the right bait. Pretty soon I had a whole collection up in my crawl space. I could go up there whenever I wanted and pick out my favorite, like some kind of lurid record collection.

Oh, and there was one other thing I found I could do. This happened totally by accident. For some reason, I've always been interested in the dents in fenders. I like to try to imagine what circumstances or objects caused the dent. I would stare at the imperfection, just like the side mirror. And, like the side mirror, if the person's thoughts were flowing in a particular manner, I would find that I could reach in and, well, snatch it. Not just any thought or desire, mind you, was available in the dented bumper. Only their happiest, freest memory. If the driver was hung up on it, dwelling, so to speak, on the happiest time of their life, and I was peering at a dent in their bumper, the memory would roll loose like a boulder, released and bound by gravity to tumble my way. I say boulder because these guys were *heavy*. I could barely get them into the house and up the stairs. Plus, they took up a lot of space.

One night I came home with the memories of a jazz pianist with arthritis in her fingers, the tender but shattered years of a mother whose son died from a fentanyl overdose, and this middle-aged guy's years of playing college hockey, only to find that the crawl space was full. Still, I couldn't stop. I had to reorganize the shed out back to make room. It was all so very interesting. I felt like I finally understood life and people. Like I had been living all this time without really understanding what made people tick. The depth of the emotions. The intensity. I organized everything into categories. Fears. Jealousies. Broken hearts. Missed opportunities. Moments that never come but always seem to be lurking around the corner. And bliss, joy. Triumphs. I had those too.

And these possessions had a strange effect on me: I finally didn't feel so alone. Riding along in traffic, I felt like part of a herd of creatures limping home from a day in the fields, trying to scrape together enough to live on. Sometimes I would be sitting at my desk as the clock approached five, and I would check the traffic and, seeing that it was light, would make up some excuse not to drive home. I would putter around the office, make small talk with the custodian, take a walk around the block, knowing that the traffic was building, building.

Or if I saw there was an accident, it would give me a little boost of anticipation. I would find myself riding down the elevator with eagerness for the clogged on-ramp and people cutting me off. Yes, yes, I would think, bubbling with joy. Go ahead. Jump onto that silver ribbon of dreams and fill it up. Jam it beyond capacity. Yes. Like some frothy, foamy enticing drink overflowing from a goblet. I would lick my lips. The on-ramps, two vehicles per green light. Just two. Like little drops of sweetener being squeezed into a giant river. But the vehicles, now that I had this newfound ability, were no longer insignificant or a burden to me. They represented possibility, a new taste or experience.

I no longer listened to books on tape, music, podcasts, or the news. My skills sharpened, improved. I prowled the lanes. My ability to penetrate mirrors and dents heightened. I could quickly ascertain if the motorist harbored a great lie, a tremendous loss, a dream of astonishing tenderness, or a dear memory.

And just as swiftly, I could detect if the driver had never really lived, or had lived a shallow life, or had never really dared to be their authentic self. I threw those back, finding them not worth my time. The side mirrors offered them to me with astonishing clarity and quickness.

One last thing: It only worked if the motorist was alone. I learned quickly that I could never penetrate a side mirror of a car with a passenger. It was closed. The driver had to be alone. I figured it had something to do with the wavelengths of lonely thoughts, which I've heard are quite long indeed.

I wish I could tell you that it went on like that. That I continued to collect, and my collection deepened into a real treasure. But, this was not the case.

One night I was washing the usual mountain of dishes when he showed up in the reflection of my kitchen window. I'll call him Boris. (That's not his real name, but out of respect for the dead and his family, I'm giving him a pseudonym.)

Boris appeared just beyond my reflection, in the shadow of my reflection, if you will. And maybe it's true that my own thoughts opened some kind of portal, some kind of back door for the people I had stolen from. That's my only explanation. Perhaps I'm as far off as the ancients that thought the earth was the center of the universe.

Boris wasn't too happy that I had taken his dream. He had wanted to be a skier, a long jumper. And he was good, very graceful. He soared through the air like a bird. They called him the Eagle. He had practiced for years, trained for the Olympics, the whole thing. Then, right before his Olympic tryout, he broke his leg. It happened when he was quite young. It was a freak thing: a little gust of air drifted over him when he wasn't expecting it, and he lost his balance. He crashed hard and shattered his leg. By the time it had fully healed, he was too old. Or felt he was too old. In the years that followed, the feeling of flying, gliding over the earth—that never went away for him.

I was scrubbing a crusty pan when he came at me. He was angry. *How dare you?* his face said. Fortunately, I knew right where it was. I was very organized. I went up to the storage closet in the attic and found it in a bin of broken dreams. I remembered just where I had left it. Boris wasn't too happy with me, but once he got his dream back, he went away.

So instead of the normal mindlessness or daydream, I started to be more aware during my nightly stack of dishes. I kept one eye on the suds, the other out the window. Sure enough, the very next night a painter showed up who had had a very sad childhood, then a brief period of intense happiness, followed by a sudden plummet back to sorrow. His parents had died when he was young. He moved in with an aunt whose neighbor taught him to paint. He developed into an astonishing artist, but doubt plagued him his whole life, like a shadow. I had his memories of learning to paint with someone who must have been his aunt's secret lover. It's a little fuzzy. My best guess is that his uncle found out about his aunt's clandestine relationship and that ended his painting education. I'm afraid the uncle was quite rough with him. He stopped painting and lived most of his life harboring a secret talent. He finally started painting in what appears to be his mid-sixties. That's when our paths crossed. He drove around in his old van with all his paintings, thinking he was going to sell them or display them, but he never did.

I remember how it all slipped right through the back window of his van. The glass had been broken and he had duct-taped a cardboard square over it, making an X and a big + with the silver tape. In the top left quadrant, the tape had slipped free. The loose end flapped and dangled in the breeze. Grabbing his memory was like peeling open a package. The joy was incredible, his childlike wonder and learning, exploring color and form, all under a well-trained eye. His mind was a sponge, soaking up everything his teacher offered.

I was sad to lose his childhood joy.

A spirit didn't come every night, more like once every two weeks. They would show up, some angry, some not. But every one of them wanted their dream or memory or desire back. No problem. As I mentioned, I was very organized. Sometimes I would have to go to the garage. Sometimes the shed. Sometimes to a storage space I had rented. In that case, I wouldn't be able to go right away. I would have to tell them to come back tomorrow and then make up some excuse to leave extra early the next morning. Some of the ghosts were impatient, others not so much. But they all had one thing in common: They wanted it back, whatever it was that I had taken.

Until Alice. That's what I'll call her. Alice had the precious gift of imagination. From a young age, she conjured up stories, poems, entire worlds, all without the slightest effort. She created complex characters and intricate plots, stories *drenched* with feelings, as easily as pulling a string or mastering some child's toy like a yo-yo. She played with words like Shakespeare, a wonder, a miracle of the human brain. But life had dropped a damn in the way. I couldn't see what it was. Some obstruction blocked her before she could get any of the stories out. She lived with all these words and lines and plots and characters all bottled up inside her while she lived her ordinary, dreary life.

I was crestfallen when she showed up in my kitchen window. I didn't want to give back her stories. She wasn't mad or impatient. She just stood there, waiting, as if in line at the grocery store, like she had stood and waited her whole life.

She wasn't in a hurry, so I didn't rush. I finished the dishes and swept the floor and wiped down the table and got the kids in bed before heading up to the attic. I had kept her stories in a special cabinet, one with all our kids' old toys that we didn't throw away. One with a lock. I kept the keys in a special drawer. The other keys on the ring were all utility keys. Backup car keys, a key to the side door of the garage, keys to the file cabinet where we kept all our financial records. These kinds of keys.

I went to the drawer, but the keys were missing. That's when I remembered: Lucy, my youngest, had been playing with the keys. She was four. She used them to pretend to start her toy car. Her car had a switch, but she wanted to do things like mommy and daddy. Everything. And she drove that thing all over the neighborhood.

The next morning was a Saturday. After searching the house and the yard and even the street, the keys were nowhere to be found. I lay awake, thinking about all those places that they could be.

I overslept a little bit. My wife yanked me out of bed. We had a busy day ahead: soccer and gymnastics and a violin recital, plus shopping for the week, new light bulbs for the bathroom, and a new screen for the screen door. The flies were getting out of hand.

"Have you seen the extra keys?" I asked my wife, busy digging out shin guards.

"What? Why do you need them right now?" she said.

"I just couldn't find them. I think Lucy was playing with them."

"They'll turn up," she said. "Can you get the waters and the shade?"

Lucy was mowing down a stack of waffles.

"Lucy, have you seen Daddy's keys?"

Lucy smiled. Her face was covered in syrup.

"The ones for your car."

"I don't know," she said.

The day was a blur. We got everything done. I saw Alice in the window. She seemed to understand that they were missing. I did my best to assure her that they would be found. They would turn up. They had to.

The next day, Sunday, we had some time in the afternoon.

"Let's go for a ride," I told her. "Take me to Daddy's keys."

Lucy got all her stuffed animals and set them in her little toy car. I followed her on my bike. She had a whole little world on our street. Where she worked. The store. The places she had to take her stuffies. We went all over, me riding behind her.

We didn't find them. We drove all over, twice, three times. That night, Alice, in her window, seemed to sense my desperation. I realized, wherever she was going, she couldn't go without her stories. I saw the same melancholy, tired look that I remembered seeing framed in her side mirror.

"They have to be somewhere," my wife said. "If not, we have originals for everything. We can just have more made."

"What about the attic cabinet? The one with all the kids' baby stuff. Do we have another key for that?"

"Hmm … I don't think so. Can't you just pry it open?"

"I suppose I could," I said. "It's just, the things in there, the old photographs and blankets and clothes and things … they're delicate. I wouldn't want to damage them."

"Why? What do you need so bad?" she asked.

"I don't. I … we … you know … need to be able to get them when we need them," I said.

I rode around with Lucy again. We went to places she had never been, just in case. We searched the house, opening all the little places and things that she could tuck something into. I stayed up late, turning the whole house inside out, even looking in places with little to no chance of having the key.

Obscure drawers, high shelves, bathroom cupboards, towel closets. I walked the neighborhood at night with a flashlight. Another week went by. Alice was starting to fade in the kitchen window.

It was a Saturday. "Grab the folding chairs," my wife said.

In the garage, the chairs were stuck. Tangled together. Lucy was crying, right by my feet, her fingers sticky from syrup. In the house, the older kids were fighting over a pair of socks.

"GOSH DARNIT!!!!" I yelled and yanked the chairs free. The utility keys came flying out. They jangled in the air and hit the ground with a tiny clang. Lucy must have put them in the chair that first Saturday.

I gave Alice her stories that night. She was little more than a thin shade. She flared bright, like a firework, before disappearing.

The next day, with the traffic heavy and the sun setting in the ocean, I didn't look at dents or side mirrors. I kept my eyes locked on the car in front of me. I drove slow, on and off the brake, listening to music, a podcast, the news, then finally some book that almost put me to sleep. It was a long ride.

It went on like that for a few weeks. I decided silence was best for the rush hour and kept my eyes on the smooth mottled gray concrete corduroy of the road. I scavenged for splotches of oil, winding cracks, or harsh skid marks.

One night I pulled into the driveway at dusk and Lucy was sitting in her little car, waiting for me.

"Can we go out and look for the keys again, Daddy?"

"But we found them," I said. "We found the keys, Lucy, remember? They were in the chair."

She sat blinking at me, not remembering or not understanding, like the keys were all part of some game.

"Can we go look for them? Please?"

She pleaded with her eyes and a pouty lower lip.

"Oh, all right," I said. "Sure. Let me put down my work bag."

"Yeah! Thanks, Daddy."

Her face broke into a wide grin as she tooted her little toy horn.

I came back out. "OK, let's go find those keys."

JOHN'S GARAGE: AN ACKNOWLEDGEMENT

"Here, do you want to hit this?" John asked me, holding out a joint.

"No thanks," I said. "I practice moderation when it comes to intoxicating my narrators."

"Makes sense," he said. He was a big guy, big beard, big stomach, strong meaty arms. Long brown hair flowed out of his black baseball hat. He was like Southern California's version of a viking.

We sat in two folding chairs in his bump-out garage, listening to Alice In Chains. He had converted it to a workshop for his knife business. Tools lined his workspace: a forge, an anvil, hammers, tongs, vises, hacksaws—basically every tool imaginable. Various knives in different stages littered the bench. It smelled like weed and metal. Beyond our chairs, there was clutter: a broken guitar, skateboards in various phases of development, an air pump, a generator, a surfboard, an old bicycle, boxes galore, and shelves lined with an eclectic collection of dusty beer bottles.

"So you're a writer?" he asked, blowing out a big toke.

"Yep," I said. "Trying to be. It's a tough business to break into."

"Probably a lot like the knife business," he said. He coughed and took a swig from his beer. "But as long you build a quality knife, things will work out. What type of writing do you do?"

"Different kinds," I said. "Fiction, short stories, some nonfiction, essays, journalism. I'm working on a couple of novels."

"I'm the same way," he said. "The pocketknife is my bread and butter. But I love to tinker. Utility knives, hunting knives, kitchen knives … switchblades, ballistic knives. I just made my first cleaver."

"A cleaver. Cool," I said.

"My point is, you can dabble and focus at the same time," he said. "Just like I do."

I nodded and tried to think of something to say.

"So you doing it all alone?" he asked. A bit of either the joint paper or weed was on his tongue, he pulled it off with his thick fingers, making little *pphhhhthh* sounds.

"Well, I'm self-publishing, but a lot of people are helping me, too," I said.

"Again. Just like building a knife," he said. "I got a steel guy, a leather guy, a guy that does stitches for me; I got a website guy, a fastener guy, a tanger guy, a butt guy— now my butt guy, that's a funny story …"

His Alice In Chain playlist ended and some hard, heavy metal came on. It was too loud, so he stood to lower the volume on the stereo. When he sat back down, he took a small hit and appeared to forget about his story.

"I'm the same way," I said. "Well not exactly. I don't have a butt guy. But I *do* have a writers group—two actually—the San Marcos Writers Group (special thanks to Wanda McLaughlin, author of *Dry Desert Heat*) and one with San Diego Writers Ink; I have a superlative and dedicated editor in Nimmy Dumm from Aspen Root Editing; I have an amazing cover designer in Jessica Bell. I owe a huge thank you to Amie McCracken (no relation to Weaver) for typesetting."

John took another hit. The garage was full of smoke.

"I have so many people to thank for my writing," I went on. "From my teachers and my family, to the authors that have inspired me, the list could on and on. I even feel a debt of gratitude for individual stories, like Vietnam vets for my Phuc's garage story."

"I feel the same way about my knife making," John said. "You take a basic blade like a clip-point, now that takes time to master. I had a teacher, guy everyone called Wick. His workshop was full of candles. He'd kick you right out if you blew out one of his candles. He had this whole thing about controlling your body and your breath in his workshop. Man, one time my friend Chad got booted for sneezing. Funniest shit. But yeah, I see what you mean. I owe a lot to Wick. Taught me a lot about sharpening metal."

"I want to thank Bewildering Stories for publishing "The Spoons of Jupiter" in 2018."

"Chad's sneeze was just a little squeaker, but it still knocked out like three flames," John said.

The heavy metal song ended. He took one last hit and put out the roach in an ash tray. It got quiet. John scratched his beard and yawned. He took another swallow and shook out the last few drops of his beer. "Well, I guess we're about through here."

We stood up and simultaneously stretched. I took a step for the door.

"Wait," I said. "Before I go, I have to thank the reader."

"Sure, go right ahead."

"Thank you reader. With all my heart."

We sat in silence for a few moments. A car drove by outside, going fast. Likely the teenager down the street.

"Have I told you about the dagger I'm making?" John asked.

"No. I don't think you have."

"Well, what's your hurry? Sit the hell down."

I complied. He opened another beer.

"It's based on a 17th century French rapier. It's unbelievably light, like a feather. Here, let me show you."

www.ingramcontent.com/pod-product-compliance
Lightning Source LLC
Chambersburg PA
CBHW021153310726
48971CB00002B/622